TANCREDI

TANCREDI

James Palumbo

MARLBOROUGH
PRESS

First published in 2011 by
Marlborough Press
103 Gaunt Street, London SE1 6DP

A catalogue record for this book
is available from the British Library

ISBN 9781908631008

Published by Emma Pickard
Typeset by Louise Ang

Printed and bound in Great Britain by
St Ives, Westerham Press

CONTENTS

I

TANCREDI SETS OFF TO SAVE THE WORLD

O nce upon a time, in the not too far distant future, there lived a young man called Tancredi who didn't conform to the conventions of the world in which he lived. This was just as well, as Earth was in a dire situation. All the planet's inhabitants suffered from the incurable disease of short-term thinking. Its symptoms were the ceaseless grabbing for gain and gratification. Although the fruits of this behaviour were rendered meaningless by death, no one could conceive of any other way of living.

On the day Tancredi was born, scientists discovered a new star. It was so small it had gone unnoticed for millennia. Stargazers named it Surprise, in the spirit of a little astrological joke. On closer inspection they made another finding, this one less amusing. After a lifetime of obscurity the diminutive star intended to draw attention to itself. Activity on its surface indicated that one day it would go supernova. A star, so insignificant it had escaped detection, was destined to be the instrument of Armageddon across the Universe.

Tancredi was raised by an uncle, who was an elegantly dressed, upstanding citizen, but mean-spirited. His parents had been inventors, killed in a space accident. Their deaths had an unusual effect on Tancredi: he became acutely aware of his own mortality. This went beyond a psychological reaction to the loss of his parents. Tancredi realised that since death was inevitable, he might as well try to achieve something in life. From this he developed a mission – he would save the planet, an objective of unthinkable altruism.

Meanwhile, his uncle had calculated that if Tancredi had inherited his parents' ingenuity, he might profit with a new wardrobe.

The teenager locked himself in his room, littering it with strange drawings and mathematical calculations. Tancredi had no friends. Birthdays and school were forgotten by the sartorial miser; both were an expense. Tancredi was indifferent to pleasure, hardly ate, never spoke except to his dog. His sole aim was to find a means to accomplish his quest. He began with a series of inventions.

His first creation reflected his struggle to find meaning in a world obsessed with the quick and easy. The CrapOmeter was a machine programmed to identify myriad word combinations bearing the reek of excrement, its function to hold a mirror to the face of man's conceits. On identification of an offending phrase, it sang out: 'Crap Warning!' But it was not a success, as mankind was addicted to this form of communication.

His uncle was beset with worry. Had his investment in the child been unwise?

Oblivious to these concerns, the young inventor persisted in his experiments. He adapted the device to serve an even higher purpose. Worn on an arm strap, the MoronOmeter acted as an eye into the world of its user. It too had a warning function. If the user was doing something moronic, like watching reality TV, a voice intoned: 'Moron! Stop it!'

Much to Tancredi's surprise, and his uncle's delight, the machine was a sell-out, but not for the reasons he might have wished. Although the MoronOmeter was intended as a life-enhancing technology, it actually encouraged the behaviour it sought to prevent.

Just as pigs love filth, morons revel in their condition. The global brotherhood of swearers, alcoholics, drug takers and trouble makers were at last united with a purpose – who could be the most moronic? Foulness was now something at which to excel. Soon there was a Moron Master League, in which armies of the professionally unemployed battled to secure the honorific conferred by his machine.

Tancredi was now in his prime, a light-heavy-weight with rimless inventor's glasses perched on a handsome face, and thick hair falling in every direction. Although his uncle had spent most of the profits from his invention on silk kimonos and exotic linens, Tancredi had enough left to buy a ticket on a space ship making its maiden voyage to the stars. He was terrified at the prospect of the journey, but knew there was no choice. Earth was a temple of expediency dedicated to the god of thoughtlessness. He must travel to fulfil his task.

Inexperienced and unsupported, the best he could do was launch himself in what might be the right direction. He hoped that determination, along with a little good fortune, would get him to where he needed to go. It was a troubled but purposeful young man who said goodbye to his uncle and the feckless people of Earth.

II
THE SPACE SHIP
INVINCIBLE

Tancredi looked up at the immensity of the ship's pin-shaped hull, a grey sea of shining metal dotted with windows and escape pods. He performed a somersault on the spot. Silly behaviour was the best antidote to anxiety. Before him was the spectacular vista of the mast, skyscraper-tall, disappearing into space. How would the monster get airborne?

Despite the size of the *Invincible*, embarkation was through a tiny portal set into its side, through which passengers were obliged to crawl on their bellies. It would take hours for everyone to board.

'Pirates, Sir,' said the ship's First Officer, noticing Tancredi's look of bewilderment. 'When everyone's in, pins will be set into the inner door as part of the ship's state-of-the-art defence system.'

'That's ridiculous.'

'Not at all. It's the latest technology. Our Astro-Voyager is the first to use it. When we're all happily boarded, you'll see how it works. You'll be amazed

6

by the beauty of the system. Simplicity combined with complexity to create harmonious unity.'

He beamed with the delight of somebody who has just recited a stock answer for the first time.

The First Officer went on to explain that pirate ships roamed space assessing the defences of target vessels. If a ship was too well-defended, the pirates would leave it alone. The *Invincible* was equipped with millions of undulating pins, attached to her inner hull. So long as they vibrated in unison, the ship was rendered invisible. The circuit was completed at the passenger door, where a guard was posted to defend against sabotage.

'When we get airborne you'll feel a jolt as the system engages,' he continued, wiggling his hips to illustrate the point. 'The pins will be undulating in harmony, and we'll disappear completely. Poof! We'll be undetectable.'

His hand swept the air like a conjurer performing a vanishing trick.

Tancredi felt nervous as he squeezed himself through the portal. In his eagerness to escape one mad world, was he crawling into another?

He inched along a tunnel, emerging into an atrium the size of a cricket pitch. His anxiety was not calmed by what he found – his fellow passengers in an ecstasy of whoops, claps and cheers, worshipping the ship's invincibility. Some were performing a can-can for no discernible reason.

Suddenly, Tancredi felt a blow to the back of his head. He had been hit by the slide section of a trombone. A band consisting of trombones, bass tubas, piccolos and kettle drums was marching up and down the deck, playing a single note. The bandsmen wore yellow costumes, with helmets from which sprouted gigantic 'I's. They were followed by a troupe of cheerleaders dressed in similar garb. The girls high-kicked and careened in every direction, linked arms and chanted:

'Invincible! Invincible! Yes! We're invincible!'

In their train appeared a trolley filled with all kinds of memorabilia, from little models of the ship to lollipops in the shape of the defensive pins. There was no short-term thinking here.

Presently, Tancredi turned his attention to a giant screen in the atrium. This showed the figure of the Captain, a man of Italian origin named Pizza, bustling about the ship's control room with all the gravitas of his position.

He appeared to be making adjustments to the ship's instruments. The room was, in fact, a stage set: the *Invincible* was operated by the Captain's thoughts.

'Welcome, spees cruisers,' Pizza boomed through a speaker, 'to the inaugural voyage of the *Invincible*, the safest ship in the univairs!'

Urged on by the band, the passengers cheered, and cries of '*Invincible!*' rang out.

'Soon we begin our spees hadventure.'

He turned towards a panel with a button set in its centre.

'As I press this button – *Avanti! La!* We go!'

The passengers gave another cheer, and awaited the moment of lift-off.

The button, of course, did nothing. The Captain pushed it with a flourish and thought 'Go'. Immediately the *Invincible*'s engines roared into life. Tancredi felt the deck vibrate beneath his feet. This was the bad part, take-off, that feeling of airlessness, of being an insignificant dot in a giant flying capsule.

Tancredi considered grabbing hold of a deck rail, then remembered a calming technique he'd invented. He began to tap the side of his nose with his index finger, telegraphing a soothing message to his brain. As the vibrations worsened, his tapping became more intense.

'Time to activate our new technology. Pin defence mechanism, engage!'

With this, the screen showed a picture of the First Officer. He had taken his place alongside the Captain and other senior crew on stage. Sure enough there was a jolt, then the officers performed a synchronised wiggle for good effect.

The passengers gawped as the picture on the screen changed to one of the vessel. As the monster moved upwards, Tancredi saw a cloud of space vapour

cascade from its fiery engines. Just as the ship reached the doorway to space,
it hung in the air, as if uncertain what to do. Suddenly the
screen went blank.

'Ha! Now we're invisible.
Per favore, enjoy
the trip.'

III

TAMANY'S

STORY

Tancredi was enjoying the view of the stars on deck when a couple approached him to ask whether he had seen their son Tamany. He was seven, small for his age with blonde hair, wearing a blue-and-white-striped top. Tamany had a galaxy of freckles and glasses just like his. They didn't seem too concerned. Tancredi looked blank.

'Keep an eye out for him, will you?' they asked, and ambled off without waiting to learn whether he would.

Momentarily the ship shuddered. To Tancredi's alarm, a crack opened in its mast which shortly expanded into a hole. He considered another somersault, but the deck was vibrating too violently to be sure of a safe landing. Instead, he went over to investigate the damaged area. A few moments later, a young boy fell through the hole, landing at Tancredi's feet. He dusted himself off, looking guilty.

'I'm so sorry,' cried Tamany, his eyes filling with tears. 'I think I've done something terrible.' He began to shake.

This was an unexpected twist. The word 'sorry' was unknown in the human lexicon. Tancredi picked the child up, carried him to a quiet corner, and sat him down. He much preferred children to adults, and felt almost compelled to comfort him.

'Don't worry, I'm sure it wasn't your fault. Tell me what you think you've done, I might be able to help.'

Tamany had never been spoken to in this way before. He blinked and looked up into the large brown eyes focussed on him. There was something about Tancredi which he trusted. He took a breath of air and began his story.

'I was a mistake, as my parents never tire of telling their friends. It took ages for me to be born – I guess I knew I wasn't wanted. Also, my bones are soft, I'm like a mouse. Wherever my head fits the rest of me follows, which is just as well. I've spent my life hiding.

'When I was three, I disappeared up our fireplace on deck. I loved the silence and secrecy. After that I followed our dog down a rabbit hole. My parents were busy, they pretended to care, but I knew they didn't.

'I hate this ship. From the moment we arrived I wanted to vanish. It was easy giving my parents the slip, they were watching that silly band march up and down. I found a hatch in the deck,' he pointed vaguely towards a corridor marked 'No Entry', 'and squeezed in.

'I went along a passage to a shaft with a ladder going up it. I looked up and saw lights fading into darkness. I began to climb. Soon I was sweating. It was getting really difficult. Would I make it to the top?

'I lost track of time after a while. My arms were getting heavy and my legs turned to stone. I thought I wasn't going to make it. I wanted to climb back down, but I didn't have the strength. Maybe I could rest on the ladder? I squeezed myself between two rungs. Next thing I knew, I was waking up.

'I felt dizzy, and the lights were out of focus. "No," I thought, "I can't pass out." I thought I saw something above me. I blinked. There was definitely something up there. It sort of shimmered, I couldn't resist it. I started climbing.

'At the top, the shaft opened into a huge dome. It was the most beautiful thing I've ever seen — a silver sea. It moved like a wave, tinkling like a wind chime. I climbed a bit higher to take a closer look.

'Then I saw what it was — millions of tiny pins. I was so close I could touch them. I wanted to stroke my hand through the sea of pins. It was so shiny. It was worth the climb — I would remember the adventure forever. Then a thought popped into my head.

'I stretched out a hand towards a pin.'

IV
THE PIRATES
ATTACK

Ten seconds after Tamany removed the pin, the *Invincible* became visible and a Nunscrut pirate ship appeared at its side. The pirate Captain was in a bad mood: he had had a dyspeptic morning trying to digest a flesh-free breakfast. He couldn't believe his luck, but the situation was clear – the ship ahead was defenceless. He belched an excited order for an immediate attack.

The *Invincible* pleasure cruiser, the pride of its line, was hit by two Nunscrut high-powered lazar torpedoes on the first day of its maiden voyage. A fissure opened in its hull, and dozens of passengers hurtled into oblivion. The ship's emergency system activated, lights flashed, a horn sounded. The pirate Captain licked his lips in pleasurable anticipation of his prize and the improved nourishment for his table. Gigantic Nunscrut harvesting nets were deployed to gather any stray proteins which might be sucked into space.

Tancredi heard the dull thud of the missile impact and was overcome by fear. This was it, the worst was about to happen. Death, dissatisfied with taking his parents, was about to engulf him as well. As the ship disintegrated, there would be a terrible sensation of falling through air. He'd be sick as his stomach turned inside out. Then he'd be ejected into blackness, human debris amongst the ship's exploding parts. He would suffocate as the *Invincible*'s oxygen supply failed.

Tancredi's finger sought the solace of his nose. Tamany looked up at his distressed companion. The child was calm, serene even. Tancredi took a deep breath; the better part of him, the Tancredi who sought to differentiate himself from the swirling mass of humanity, took control. He would face the danger, and find a way out.

He began to analyse the situation. Despite his awareness of mankind's addiction to short-termism, he expected some signs of concern from his fellow shipmates. He had read accounts of the last hours of the *Titanic*, whose passengers regarded the evacuation as sport. They perambulated its decks, listened to the band, and even as the water lapped their feet, poured more drinks. He thought of his uncle, who would be horrified to get his clothes wet. He wondered at what point the passengers of the *Titanic* had realised they were going to die. Was it on contact with the water?

The lessons of history were clear. It was human nature not to face facts until it was too late. People would continue to watch reality TV even as a clock on screen counted down to Armageddon. After all, what better show than one's own destruction?

He peered out of the space window. There were corpses floating outside, visible to anyone looking. Nunscrut harvesting nets wafted through space snaring the bodies. But the mass of the passengers continued to glue their collective focus on the big screen. Perhaps he was overreacting. His ability to see through to the gruesome end was a quality, but what was the dividing line between prudence and paranoia? Could it be that one person among thousands was right? And if he was, would he follow his own opinion or run with the pack?

'Don't you think you should get to an escape pod?' he said to a man holding a beer bottle nearby, enjoying the show.

'Why?' the man replied. 'The ship's invincible, isn't it? Anyway, the Captain hasn't said anything.'

Tancredi picked up a pair of cheerleader pom-poms discarded on the deck. He jumped up and down in imitation of a hornpipe dance, waving the pom-poms in the man's face.

'Panic! Panic! Panic!' he screeched. 'What about those bodies?' He gestured at the floating corpses. 'Don't you feel something's wrong?'

The beer drinker looked at him wearily, barely bothering to move his head.

'None of my business. Anyway, who's to say what they are? Perhaps they're foreign bodies? Perhaps they've gone for a space walk?'

At this, a nearby passenger opened his mouth, raised his eyebrows in anticipated pleasure, and looked around at his fellow travellers.

17

'Space walk!' he exclaimed, and laughed loudly.

It seemed to be contagious, everyone nearby cried 'Space walk!' and collapsed with laughter. Shortly, the entire deck was laughing, this was the funniest joke ever.

Incredible, thought Tancredi, collective euphoria without an ounce of humour. As for the beer drinker, would he clutch the bottle to him, perhaps taking a final sip as he was sucked into space?

'Come on, Tamany,' he said, grabbing his little hand, 'let's go and see if we can find your parents.'

For a moment Tamany looked downcast, then he recovered and trotted along beside Tancredi.

Having immobilised the cruiser with his torpedoes, the Nunscrut Captain calculated his men had several hours in which to board and plunder the ship. By the time it floundered, he would be counting his spoils.

Captain Pizza knew that the *Invincible* had been delivered a fatal blow; it was only a matter of time before she exploded. He was also aware of his duty – to race about the ship overseeing its evacuation, before sharing in its final disintegration. Yet he, too, was a student of self-interest, in this instance his own salvation. As the Captain made for an escape pod, the words 'Free!' and 'Quick!' popped unbidden into his head.

The fissure had opened to the size of a house. The ship's computer was beginning to malfunction. In its digital delirium, it somehow connected these words to the Captain's name, then improvised on the theme. As the *Invincible* began to list, a message flashed across the video screen:

'Free! Pizza! Quick while it's hot! Free! Spicy hot!'

The effect on the passengers was instantaneous. No show was complete without a snack break. There was a headlong rush to the ship's galleys.

Tancredi and Tamany arrived at the ship's atrium. There would be time to evacuate later; as far as he could see, not a single escape pod had been used. He confronted a scurrying passenger with his pneumatic pom-poms.

'Don't you want to escape? The ship's about to explode.'

'Free pizza! Quick! Free pizza! Spicy and hot! Free pizza!' the passenger replied.

Tancredi was amazed. Gratification was one thing, but the price of this pizza was death. He imagined a trail of slippery saliva all the way to the quick-food galleys. There was nothing he could do for his fellow passengers: it was time for him and Tamany to make their escape.

Two hours after the Nunscrut torpedoes struck the *Invincible*, the fissure in her side opened like a zip. With the sputtering of its motors, the ship began to lose stability. One minute the passengers found themselves floating in the air, the next they were dumped on the floor. Hundreds were catapulted into space, as denial finally gave way to panic.

V

THE END OF
THE LINE

In place of the promised pizza, the video screens now displayed a clock. This showed minutes, seconds and fast-running milliseconds, counting down to oblivion. A soothing voice rang out, 'Ship will destruct in five minutes.'

Tancredi noticed that the announcement had a mixed effect on the passengers. Some were whipped into a state of panic, others took it as a source of continued entertainment and gathered before the screen to watch and laugh at the chaos unfolding.

Tancredi and Tamany moved on and arrived at a bank of escape pods where a confused-looking crowd had gathered. They were rapping on the pod doors as if this would open them. Tancredi understood the problem. The ship's power had failed; there was no way they could be unlocked.

Tancredi had always felt he would have survived the sinking of the *Titanic* without displacing a woman or child in a lifeboat. It was a matter of facing facts – there would have been time to build a raft and escape the stricken boat. Now he was on the deck of his own *Titanic*, and he had failed. Who was the fool now?

His instinct had warned him to escape immediately, yet he had faltered. Hadn't he prided himself on being able to see what others couldn't?

And now, for all his high-mindedness, he found himself in the same situation as everyone else. In these last moments, he felt an odd kinship with the pizza eaters. When it's time to go, you all go down together.

The deck began to buckle, the air became thin. He looked at Tamany. In his idiocy he was responsible for leading a child to this fate. He struck at a window in impotent rage, cutting his hand. Blood began to pour from the wound.

'Ship will destruct in three minutes.'

'I can fit through,' said a small voice.

Tancredi examined the child. It was impossible, but what other options were there? He was astonished by what happened next. Tamany jumped up and forced his head through the opening, followed by his trunk, then his legs, kicking as he went through.

'Push the open button!' Tancredi shrieked. 'It must be there – find it!'

'It's not here, I can't see ...' said a disembodied voice. 'Maybe ...'

The door swung open. Tancredi charged forwards, sweeping the child contortionist into his arms. The reassuring voice announced, 'Ship will destruct in one minute – you are advised to make your way to an escape pod at your earliest convenience, thank you.'

Tancredi took the controls. A man of science, he understood how to operate the machine, including the emergency drive. Anything near the mother ship would be vaporised when she exploded. He fired the engine. Instantly a message flashed on the control panel: 'Malfunction, insert pin to re-set system.' Tancredi scanned the panel and saw a microscopic hole beside the words 'Insert pin here'.

'No! No! No!' cried Tancredi, striking the panel, 'Where on earth am I going...' He stopped mid-sentence.

There were seconds to go before oblivion. Now that death was certain, a strange euphoria washed over him. He closed his eyes and tilted back his head. However short, his adventure had been worth it. He would die a doer. Suddenly he felt uncomfortable. He'd prefer to stride towards death, rather than sit plaintively waiting for the axe to fall. He looked at his little friend and stretched out a hand – they'd face it together. Tamany showed no fear, he appeared to be thinking hard.

'Ten seconds ...'

Tamany plucked at his sleeve, eyes fixed on the panel. There was a silver flash in the air, then the sound of an engine humming as his precious pin hit the circuit in the spot specified.

Tancredi flushed red as a demon spirit possessed him. He blew the space door, set the engine to full and pushed forward all at the same time.

'Five, four...'

The pod detached from the mother ship.

'Three, two...'

'Go! Go! Go!' shrieked Tancredi, punching the emergency drive.

'One...'

There was a bang, a flash,
then a million stars
sped by in slow
motion.

VI

THE BATTLE OF THE LIVING DEAD

As injuries were often sustained in emergency evacuations, the escape pod was programmed to carry its passengers to the nearest world with medical facilities. It analysed the options and found a suitable planet. The pod came to rest with a gentle shudder on the summit of a verdant knoll in bright sunlight.

The control panel showed Tancredi he had landed on Sanitalis, a health planet devoted to the well-being of mankind. His heartbeat was beginning to slow following his brush with death. He felt braver. He had saved Tamany and piloted the craft from the exploding ship without so much as a single tap of his nose. Although he knew the journey ahead would be long, he felt he'd survived a rite of passage. He was also cheered to have landed on Sanitalis. After the nihilism of Earth and the horrors of the *Invincible*, here at last was a civilisation based on the far-sighted philosophies of care and compassion.

Tamany was similarly in a better mood. He might have been responsible for the destruction of the ship, but his pin had saved their lives. His pride in this achievement soothed his remorse over the fate of the *Invincible*. Tancredi dreaded bringing up the subject of his parents, but was amazed by Tamany's response.

The child admitted to being sad, he was sorry for their loss, but it would be difficult to miss them. He explained in a calm voice that he'd noticed there were all sorts of parents, from the terrific to the terrible. Since his had been at the latter end of the scale, he found it difficult to show the grief expected of him.

After a lifetime spent amongst fools, Tancredi was astonished to have found a kindred spirit in the form of a seven-year-old child.

It was a beautiful day. Birdsong filled the air. The adventurers surveyed the green countryside, stretching for miles in every direction. Tancredi splayed himself out on the warm grass, let out a deep breath and closed his eyes. He felt the warmth of the sunshine wash his face. Maybe life wasn't so bad after all. He was about to fall asleep when he heard the sound of hoarse voices. He stood up to investigate, and was shocked by what he saw.

Gathered at the foot of the hill was an army of the sick in medical robes, swathed in blood-soaked bandages. They walked with a rolling limp, some dragging mangled legs in their wake. Deformed heads sat atop numerous humps, bumps and other disfigurements, and they carried scalpels, saws and medical blades of different sorts.

Tancredi felt the old fear returning and reached for his nose. His anxiety was compounded by the fact that he didn't understand what they were doing. Tamany gazed down the hill.

'Don't worry,' he said, 'they're just sick.'

Emboldened, Tancredi decided to confront them.

'Why are you disturbing the peace of Sanitalis?' he shouted. 'This is a place of long-term thinking, dedicated to medicine.'

The army shuffled. A patient emerged from the ranks, swathed top to toe in bandages with only a slit for his mouth.

'I'm the Chief Patient,' he croaked, jerking his head in every direction, unable to see Tancredi. 'What you say is nonsense.'

He lurched a few paces forward.

'This is a place of madness. Long-term thinking is unknown in the health profession. Sanitalis is out of control. It's creating a monster which will wreck the planet.'

Tancredi was incredulous – the health profession, committed to good works, creating a monster? What was he talking about?

'Who are you? What do you want?'

'We're the sick who wish to die,' replied the Chief Patient, 'but medicine on Sanitalis requires human life to be extended indefinitely, regardless of cost.

I'm one hundred and fifty-nine years old. There are millions of us undergoing continuous surgery to prolong our lives.'

He started to unfurl his bandages to prove the point.

'The only original part of my body is my backside. Everything else has been replaced at least once. I'd been in hospital for thirty years before I escaped to join the Revolution for Death. Half the population are attached to life-support machines, incapable of doing anything for themselves. Behold the future of medicine!'

Tancredi was perplexed. Wasn't sustaining life a worthy cause? He was about to reply when Tamany tugged at his sleeve, and pointed to what appeared to be a giant speaker on wheels coming up the far side of the hill. It was accompanied by an army of unarmed middle-aged men, dressed in brown jackets with plastic identity tags which twinkled in the sunlight. They were in no rush; Tancredi could hear the strain of civilised conversation. Behind him the maimed patients wailed and moaned.

'I don't know what's going on,' Tancredi said to Tamany nervously. 'We'd better get out of the way.'

The patient army quickly deployed at the crest of the hill. As it beheld the opposing force, a banshee cry went up. The brown combatants reacted with indifference, turned their backs and continued their conversations. Some broke out flasks of tea, which they poured into plastic cups before adding milk and sugar with pedantic precision. A few attempted to drink from teaspoons with insistent pecking motions like busy woodpeckers.

This enraged the patients, and a roar of anger issued from their ranks. Tancredi expected the brown army to react, but its only point of activity was a technician busying himself at the base of the giant speaker at the front of their assembly.

The patient army stumbled forward on the battlefield. A rainstorm of scalpels and other sharp objects flew overhead, but fell short of the target of their hatred. Tancredi rushed Tamany towards the cover of a tree. He held the child behind him and peered out from around its trunk.

A single brown-clad warrior stepped out from the opposing ranks holding a microphone. His colleagues took out notepads and pens and turned to observe the shambolic horde careering towards them with heads slightly cocked in academic interest. A wave of realisation swept over Tancredi. This was an army of psychiatrists.

'Testing, testing,' said the Chief Psychiatrist.

The patient army continued its awkward charge.

Tancredi wanted to escape but couldn't; they were trapped on the brow of the hill. Tamany felt his unease via his hand and gave it a reassuring squeeze.

'Your eyes are ...' began the Chief Psychiatrist.

He was cut off mid-sentence.

'Blast,' he said turning to the technician, 'would you be so kind ...?'

The technician fumbled with some wires, then nodded his head.

'Thank you so much,' shot out of the speaker at huge decibels.

He turned once again towards the maniacal charging horde.

'Your eyes are getting heavy,' he said smoothly. As his sing-song words reverberated across the hilltop, the front rank wavered.

'Let me take you back to your childhoods, soothe you.'

Now the patients lost momentum. The charge became a trot, and some fell over in a heap. The soporific voice continued.

'Hush, that's it, relax. Let's talk this through. You know you're over-reacting to being fed by your fathers. Let your anger sweep over you. That's right.'

They shuddered to a standstill and looked about, unsure what to do. Some started to cry. A murmur of approval of the Chief Psychiatrist's technique rang out from the brown army. A few started to applaud politely in recognition of the success of the live demonstration. At this point, the Chief Psychiatrist smiled around at his admirers and began to croon into the microphone.

'Shush, little babies, you go to sleep ...'

A great sigh went up from the patients. Saws and scalpels were dropped, and those still wavering fell to the ground.

Later, the patients were escorted back to their hospital beds by a squad of nurses. Tancredi wasn't surprised that they'd succumbed to the trickery of psychiatrists; presumably they also ruled the planet. One day Earth too might be governed by a profession which fuelled people's obsession with themselves. Who better to rule than professional problem-solvers?

But Tancredi distrusted psychiatry. Wasn't it just a covert method for its practitioners to deal with their own psychoses? It was, after all, a subjective science. What if its 'proven theories' were wrong? Did boys really want to sleep with their mothers and kill their fathers?

Still, perhaps things were different on a planet dedicated to health. He approached the Chief Psychiatrist.

'That was a neat trick,' he said.

'Not at all, not at all.' The Chief Psychiatrist turned towards him with the smug satisfaction of a man who is in command of events. He had a bald head, a great beak of a nose, and continuously blinking eyes behind inch-thick glasses.

'We are the army of Sanitalis. Whenever the sick cause problems, we deal with it. With those escaped patients it was like handling a pettish child. How would they know what's good for them?'

'They say that Sanitalis is creating a monster of its own, the planet's out of control,' said Tancredi.

The Chief Psychiatrist threw back his head and laughed with delight.

'What? Devotion to medicine spawns a beast? Insanity! Our health service is beyond reproach, as you'll soon discover.'

Tancredi was about to reply when the Chief Psychiatrist pointed at his stomach. He looked down. He was the only one to have suffered an injury. He had been pierced by a flying scalpel.

VII
TANCREDI GOES TO
HOSPITAL

Tancredi was rushed to hospital in Hippocratopolis, the capital of Sanitalis. Watching the battle, he had felt a twinge in his stomach but failed to react. For someone skilled in facing reality, he was very squeamish about blood.

He had once had an operation on Earth to remove a mole from his chest. Afterwards, he was told to rest; instead he made love to a girl all night. On awakening he went to the bathroom and looked in the mirror. There was a hole in his chest where the wound had opened. He fainted on the spot. Since then he had found reasons to delay visits to dentists and doctors.

The injury was now revealed to be serious.

'I'll operate on you myself,' said the Chief Psychiatrist, grinning in anticipation of repairing an alien, 'but first I must ask you some questions – how do you feel?'

'Not good,' Tancredi replied, 'I've got a sharp pain in my abdomen ...'

'I was, in fact, asking about your inner feelings. I'd like to take you back to your earliest memories.'

'Is that really necessary?' replied Tancredi, turning green.

'Of course. Here on Sanitalis, everyone visits a psychiatrist daily as part of their long-term health needs.'

After his operation, Tancredi awoke in a berth at the end of a row of beds. Through the window, he could see a building site. The ward was magnificently furnished, with marble columns and silk curtains. Patients lay in four-poster beds with carved mahogany bedposts. Despite the pleasant surroundings, Tancredi hated hospitals and wanted to leave immediately.

Beyond this, he felt something was wrong. He was grateful for the care he'd received, but any world run by psychiatrists was, by definition, a disaster zone.

Although he didn't understand the patients' talk about a monster, he felt sure the planet was destined for a bad ending. He turned to speak to the patient in the bed next to him, and was surprised to see a dog's snout protruding from beneath the covers.

'Hello,' he said, 'are you sick?'

Tancredi was used to speaking to animals, he'd spent his childhood talking to his dog. He far preferred animals to people. As his dog grew older, he dreaded the moment of its death. When the time came he was inconsolable. For Tancredi, the definition of sadness was the death of a dog.

'What's a dog doing in hospital?' he asked an ample-bosomed Matron who had come over to nurse him.

'Now don't be ungracious, dearie,' the Matron sang in a lilting voice. 'The health service on Sanitalis is for everyone, even dogs. A dog or cat can give hours of comfort so they must be looked after or stuffed. Isn't that right, my fine fellow?' she trilled to the dog, who looked on with an anxious flutter of his brown eyes.

'But what's wrong with him?'

'Oh, nothing. He's a stray, so we thought we'd give him a quick check-up. He's called Kasbek.' She went over to pat his head. 'If nothing else you can be stuffed, can't you, my fine friend? A friend for life, that's what you'll be.'

'Amazing, even dogs are looked after. I prefer living dogs, personally,' replied Tancredi.

'Yes, well, I'll have to pass that on to the Chief Psychiatrist for analysis. Interesting comment, dearie. Stuffed they're less bother and easier to carry around. Practical. That's what you need to be, sweetie. Now let's have a good look at you.'

Tancredi expected the Matron to attend to his wound but she just stood and observed him. She brought a fleshy hand up to her chin, and a note of thoughtful reflection emanated from deep within her throat. Feeling awkward, Tancredi sought to change the object of her attention.

'What's going on outside the hospital?'

'We're just extending it,' said the Matron looking out of the window. 'We're always extending it. Extend life. Extend care. Extend medicine. That's our motto.'

With this she turned and trotted off down the ward, practising a can-can kick as she went.

A terrible noise sounded outside the window. Tancredi wanted to see what was going on. He got out of bed, suddenly aware that he was dressed in a funny back-to-front robe which exposed his posterior.

'You coming along?' he said to his neighbour.

Kasbek bounded out of bed, revealing himself to be an Irish wolfhound with a magnificent silver coat. He wagged his tail with excitement. Tancredi buried his face in Kasbek's fur, breathing in his dog smell. He stroked his head, bending back his ears, then kissed his snout. He knew they'd be friends.

Kasbek pawed at the covers of his bed. It seemed empty to Tancredi. Then the sheets folded back to reveal Tamany. He had rolled himself into a little ball and hidden in the bed with Kasbek to escape the Matron's ministrations.

'She wanted me to do this funny kicking thing,' he said.

Now he mounted Kasbek like a horse, and they trotted off down the ward. Tancredi limped beside them, clutching his bandaged wound.

Presently they found their way to the hospital roof, which gave a panoramic view of Hippocratopolis. The area around the hospital was a hive of activity. Workers were smashing houses, shops, offices, trees, fountains: anything that could be flattened was a target for destruction. Tancredi had never seen demolition on such a large scale.

'I wonder what it's all for?' Tamany asked Tancredi, who climbed up onto an empty plinth and assumed a heroic pose.

'Long-term thinking,' breathed the Chief Psychiatrist, who had sidled up to observe them on the roof, notebook in hand. 'We need more beds for patients.'

He handed Tancredi a pair of binoculars.

'Tell me,' asked Tancredi, 'why do you need all this space?'

'Because of the obese, the smokers, drug takers, and alcoholics. They all need to be accommodated, cared for and analysed, particularly analysed.'

'But is that sensible?' queried Tancredi. 'Shouldn't you be cracking down on people who don't look after themselves?'

'Are you joking?' snorted the Chief Psychiatrist, fixing Tancredi with a stare of contempt.

'A diet of pizza and beer that leads to heart disease isn't the fault of the individual – it's the failure of society. Surely you acknowledge that? It's impossible for people to take responsibility for their actions until the causes of their problems have been analysed.'

He blinked repeatedly from behind his reinforced glasses to emphasise the point.

Tancredi was beginning to understand the necessity for large-scale demolition works on Sanitalis. All that he loathed about psychiatry had also been confirmed. The planet was the living embodiment of its dubious theories. Everything was the fault of someone or something other than the individual.

He scanned the surrounding area with the binoculars and brought them to focus on the Chief Psychiatrist, who, not realising he was being watched, picked his nose. He inspected the fruit of his labour, then slipped it into a top pocket with practised grace.

'But where does it all end?' Tancredi asked, disguising his disgust. 'Won't the system spiral out of control?' The image of a monster on the loose flashed through his mind.

'There is no end, why should there be? As for cost, what price do you put on life? On Sanitalis, we're committed to total care, irrespective of cost. Everyone must be made well. We are a Well-Being Society.'

Tancredi returned to his bed, confused and repulsed. The Chief Psychiatrist's filthy habit had put him off the gourmet food served in the hospital ward. Beyond this, he didn't understand how such an excessive system could work. He turned on the news to learn more about the planet.

The newsreader was talking about hospital-building programmes. There wasn't just one scheme under development in Hippocratopolis: enormous swathes of Sanitalis were being flattened to make way for new facilities. A city in the north had just been destroyed to create a gigantic hospitalisation zone called 'Smokers Don't You Worry'. Tancredi nodded off to sleep.

The newsreader began an interview with a psychiatrist dressed in a brown jacket.

'I'm obliged to ask you whether the cost of this new facility is justifiable? Why should Sanitalis bear the burden when smokers are warned the habit will kill them?'

The psychiatrist shot the interviewer a look of horror.

'I find it very difficult to respond to such bigoted questions. Were you dropped on your head as a baby?'

He was about to elucidate further, when the Matron burst into the ward
like a bold Valkyrie.

'Quick!' she screamed. 'Everyone out.
The Monster is coming!'

VIII
THE MONSTER
OF SANITALIS

Tancredi was having his favourite dream. He was a human bird, soaring above grey rooftops and green fields. The view was magical. The feeling of airlessness he hated on the *Invincible* was replaced by a sense of exhilaration and excited uncertainty over how long he could sustain his flight. He felt a weightless power over the world and humankind. Suddenly he experienced himself descending; he had lost the ability to fly. He glided back down to the ground, which began to shake as he landed.

Everything was pandemonium in the ward – the marble columns were cracked, the windows splintered. Tancredi felt the old fear bubble up, but his dream gave him courage. He would survive whatever was about to happen.

Tamany appeared at his bedside. He'd been playing with Kasbek while Tancredi slept.

'I think we'd better leave,' he said, 'we'll help you out of bed.'

Kasbek jumped up and licked Tancredi's mouth in canine solidarity.

'Good idea,' said Tancredi, 'it feels like an earthquake.'

He swung his legs over the side of the bed, stood up with a groan and took Tamany's hand.

'You coming, Kasbek?' he asked.

'Don't be ridiculous,' Tamany replied. 'Of course he is.'

Kasbek sprang into the air; he understood what they were saying.

'Here dearies, follow me, follow me,' clucked the Matron, scuttling down the ward, practising another can-can kick. 'I'd better take this just in case.'

She grabbed hold of a bed pan.

'Why's she doing that funny kick?' Tamany asked. 'She keeps trying to get everyone to do it. Is it an exercise for the sick?'

'I've got no idea,' Tancredi replied. 'It's very odd, maybe we'll find out later.'

They arrived in the hospital parking lot to find the Chief Psychiatrist waiting for them in an ambulance.

'Get in,' he cried, 'we haven't much time.'

Tancredi didn't want to accept his help. He was sure the practice of his art had sent the Chief Psychiatrist mad. Still, there didn't seem to be much choice. The hospital was collapsing about their heads, and the ambulance offered a way out.

'What's happening?' he asked.

'I can't say,' replied the Chief Psychiatrist. 'I think something's wrong with our health system.'

The vibrations got worse. As the ambulance sped from the car park, a terrible groan issued from the hospital behind them. Suddenly Tancredi realised they were driving backwards.

'Why are we going in reverse?' he asked.

'I'm shocked by your question,' the Chief Psychiatrist replied. 'Don't you care about health and safety?'

'Not particularly,' Tancredi retorted.

'Health and safety on Sanitalis,' he said, turning to look at Tancredi rather than the road, 'dictates that I'm only allowed to drive backwards.'

No wonder, nonsense made sense on Sanitalis. Now Tancredi was worried for his life.

'Please watch where you're going,' he begged.

'It also dictates that the addressee must be addressed with full eye contact to avoid a paranoid reaction. But since we must leave the area, I also have to drive. Given these circumstances, I am therefore required to look at you while I drive. It's a logical conclusion to a series of empirical events. Surely you understand this?'

Tancredi glanced behind him at the hospital. It was shaking as if struck by an earthquake. Tamany, the Matron and Kasbek pressed against the window to watch. Soon the hospital began to rise into the air, but it didn't disintegrate as it moved upwards. To Tancredi's astonishment, it formed into the shape of a human leg. His finger reached involuntarily for the comfort of his nose.

There was panic on the roads. Everyone was saying: 'The Monster is coming!' There seemed to be no means of escape until the Chief Psychiatrist announced, 'Don't worry, we'll head for the coast.'

The skies darkened on the journey, not with storm clouds, but with great shapes swirling in the air.

'Look, there's a torso,' said the Matron.

'And isn't that an arm?' asked Tamany.

As the travellers looked up, the most extraordinary thing happened – the arm and torso combined.

After a short distance they found the roads blocked and the ambulance could go no further.

'Right, everybody out,' said the Chief Psychiatrist, 'we'll walk the rest of the way.'

A signpost told them they were a few miles from the coast. Every few steps the Matron practised a can-can kick.

'What's she doing?' Tancredi asked the Chief Psychiatrist, hoping he might be able to explain her erratic behaviour.

'Oh, she's practising the dance,' he replied matter-of-factly. Tancredi looked blank.

'There's a theory going around,' the Chief Psychiatrist explained. 'When Surprise goes supernova, anyone who links arms and does the can-can will be protected from the blast. Something about creating a cosmic counter-vibration. There is, however, another school of thought. This states that those who flap their arms vigorously will fly with the explosion unharmed. The can-can theory is dominant.'

Tancredi and Tamany looked at each other, stupefied. This was beyond the insanity they'd encountered on the *Invincible*.

'Dogs have to do it as well,' Tamany said to Kasbek with a chuckle. Kasbek cocked his head by way of response.

Still, the pressing issue remained the hospitals spinning above their heads.

'What about all those hospitals in the sky?' asked Tancredi pointing upwards. 'It looks as if something's out of control. I thought Sanitalis was a place of careful planning.'

'We started with the best motives,' replied the Chief Psychiatrist with a sigh, 'but somehow we got carried away. It seems that good short-term intentions have led to a bad long-term result.'

By now they had arrived at a cliff top by the coast.

'What's that?' asked Tamany, pointing out to sea at a great shape advancing.

'It's a tsunami,' replied the Matron.

'No, it's not,' said Tancredi, 'it's too big for that. It looks like a floating city.'

Kasbek began to whimper; his dog senses told him something terrible was about to happen. The little group strained to discern the composition of the approaching shape. Presently it towered over the cliff top; now they had a close-up view.

The Monster was composed of all the hospitals ever built on Sanitalis. Somehow they had torn themselves loose from their foundations, and floated off into the sky. Its limbs were made of walls; its torso from rooftops; its face, hospital beds pimpled with red brick and sash-cracked windows; its skin was linen; its eyes two liniment-filled pools. A groan came from deep within its body.

'Hush little baby, don't you ...' began the Chief Psychiatrist.

The Monster looked down at the tiny figure and grunted. Tancredi gasped. Somehow he knew what was about to happen. He grabbed Tamany and covered the boy's eyes. A great hand swung over the cliff top and caught hold of the Chief Psychiatrist. Tancredi watched in horror as the Monster stuffed him into its mouth.

'Oh my goodness,' said the Matron shaking with fear. 'Here dearie, you'd better take this.'

She handed Tancredi her bedpan, then took off on her fat legs, practising can-can kicks as she went.

Tancredi, Tamany and Kasbek were left on the cliff top. Escaping an exploding ship was one thing, but facing this Monster was on another scale. Tancredi froze, his legs turned to jelly. Tamany tore free from his grasp and leapt onto Kasbek, who reared up on his back legs.

'Come on, beast!' echoed out across the cliff top in a treble voice.

Tancredi blinked and returned to reality. He was shamed by the lesson in courage from a seven-year-old. He too would die defiant.

His fear of death was now replaced by a feeling of humiliation. Here he was on the cliff top, bedpan in hand, staring stupidly into the eyes of his killer. The horror of execution wasn't the blow itself, it was the indignity of being in someone else's hands, of penitently bending your head beneath the blade. If he could resolve to die bravely, he would be a different man during the few seconds remaining. He held up the bedpan in a gesture of defiance.

The Monster bent down to examine the group, and opened its mouth. They stared into the maw of the beast. Bedpan enamel teeth dribbled fetid juices over them. The foul smell of the putrefaction of sickness – blood, pus and gangrenous flesh – enveloped the cliff top. Miraculously, they managed to stay upright as the Monster inhaled a breath so gigantic that it sucked the air out of the atmosphere. Then it exhaled with the power of a hurricane, and Tancredi and his companions were catapulted into the starry vortex.

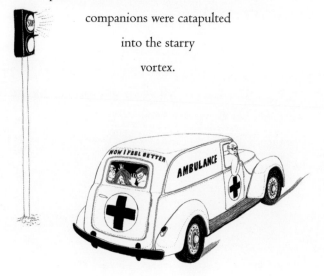

IX

THE TWIN MOONS
OF EROS

S uch was the force of the Monster's breath that the group was shot straight through space towards a neighbouring planet. They landed on soft cushions in the courtyard of a palace on the first moon of Eros. One moment Tancredi was about to be swallowed alive, the next he heard the sound of a fountain playing. He couldn't believe this act of providence. Tamany instantly forgot the Monster, picked up a cushion and accosted Kasbek. As the two began to chase around the courtyard, Tancredi went off to explore.

Despite his luxurious surroundings, Tancredi's feelings were mixed. Although he knew he hadn't conquered his cowardly tendencies, he had been brave in the face of death. He was no longer the man who had so recently left home. Still, his idealistic hopes had been dashed. He was no closer to finding a solution to Earth's predicament. Sanitalis was no more a place of long-term thinking than the *Invincible*. As for the Matron's proposed antidote to Armageddon, it seemed as if the further he travelled, the more delusional humankind became.

With these troubling thoughts in mind, he arrived at a bar. He lay on the counter, rested his head on a cushion he had purloined from the palace of bliss, and groaned. Although Tancredi had a penchant for eccentric gestures, Eros One was a pleasure moon; no behaviour was considered unusual. The barman poured the prone figure a drink and left him alone, until he noticed a girl sashay across the room in Tancredi's direction.

'Be careful of that one, Sir,' he whispered in his ear.

Tancredi raised his head and his heart began to race. A hot flush infused his body, sending a tingle to his extremities. The girl was beautiful beyond words. Long black hair fell unstyled over high cheekbones, oval black eyes and the plumpest mouth imaginable. She wore a simple red satin dress, slit to the thigh, and heels which accentuated her slim legs. On Earth, her tanned skin, soft and flawless, might have suggested Indian blood. Here it revealed that she was from the second moon of Eros.

'Hello,' she said in a husky voice, paralysing him with a synchronised flash of her eyes and beauty-queen smile. 'I'm Cocomo.'

Tancredi felt painfully inferior. As he opened his mouth to introduce himself, she slapped him hard across the face.

'Ouch,' he said in a shrill voice, bringing a hand up to his reddening cheek. 'Why did you do that?' He slipped off the counter and sat on a barstool.

52

The gorgeous creature shot him a glance of contempt.

'You look pathetic. Pull yourself together.'

Tancredi had never been slapped before, let alone spoken to in this manner. On Earth he had been successful with girls, thanks to his good looks and status as the inventor of the MoronOmeter. He wondered what might be behind this beauty's strange behaviour. Like most young men, he conjured up a reason favourable to himself.

There was a technique for seduction on Earth known as the 'neg'. It used the kind of elementary psychology of which the Chief Psychiatrist would have approved. When meeting someone desirable, the interested party feigns indifference by deploying a derogatory remark or suddenly abandoning a conversation. The rejected person is then motivated to seek the attention of the seemingly uninterested party. Cocomo's slap across the face must be a 'neg', a sign of interest.

As Tancredi comforted himself with this thought, another stunning creature walked into the bar. She was wearing a similar dress, in white silk with no slit. She flowed towards him. Her blonde hair fell in waves down to her waist. As she approached, Tancredi was transfixed by piercing blue eyes set in an angelic face.

'That's Bonnita,' the barman said, 'she's a good girl.' He cast a sideways glance at Cocomo. 'They don't like each other, something about a man.'

'Poor boy,' said Bonnita touching Tancredi's thick black hair, 'has Cocomo been nasty to you? I'm afraid it's in her nature.'

Thrilled by the goddess's attention, Tancredi leapt off his barstool.

'It's a pleasure to meet you both,' he said, then slumped down again. 'But I'm afraid I won't be good company.'

This was an attempt to elicit sympathy. His confidence had collapsed. The two most exquisite women in the Universe were standing before him. Tancredi reasoned that the game between the sexes must be played at a far higher level on this planet. He was confused and searching for ways to protect himself. Perhaps Cocomo hadn't used a 'neg'. He wasn't equipped to deal with such overwhelming beauty.

'Grow up,' said Cocomo harshly. 'I'm not falling for the "oh poor me" trick.'

Tancredi's descent into chaos continued. The chase was afoot and he was a novice compared to this hunter-killer. At this moment he wished to perform Tamany's disappearing trick, or touch the calming softness of Kasbek's coat. If pity wasn't going to work, perhaps he could try the grandiloquent statement. The one he invoked at least had the benefit of being the truth.

'I come from a faraway place,' he said, looking dejected, 'seeking to save it from destruction. I've travelled on a space ship which exploded and to a health planet which turned out to be sick. Everywhere I find people venal and foolish.

I'm beginning to despair. Is no one in the Universe thoughtful?'

'No,' Cocomo said with a laugh, 'especially not you, fool! You've come to the wrong place. Eros One is a pleasure moon dedicated to gratification. Eros Two, the planet I come from, can't solve your problem, but at least we're good at human relations.'

'Is that so?' interrupted Bonnita, 'That's an interesting concept coming from you. In what way?'

'The famous divorce ceremony, of course. Everyone who fails in marriage must undergo the ordeal. As a result people think before making the commitment, unlike here where relationships have no meaning.'

'And are you superior, given your profession?' Bonnita asked with contempt.

'As a matter of fact I am,' Cocomo replied, looking straight at Tancredi rather than her inquisitor. 'A prostitute with a mission outranks a mediocrity who thinks only about herself.'

To Tancredi's embarrassment, a prudish look spread across his face. He groped for a way forward.

'Let's have a drink,' he said. 'Tell me about yourselves.'

If he could encourage a debate between a dissolute woman and a living angel,

he might even dodge the bullets. As the girls sat down, glaring at

each other, another thought flashed unbidden through

Tancredi's mind: there was nothing to

prevent him from finding love

on his adventure.

X
COCOMO'S
STORY

I come from a good family and had an education of sorts, but we fell on hard times. My papa was a spendthrift, my mama couldn't make ends meet. At seventeen, I knew it was me against the rest of the world. I felt frightened but liberated.

'When I left home to make my fortune, I had no intention of doing this job. I wanted to use my looks to work as a bar hostess, make big tips, save money. Immediately men began to bother me like flies around dung. At first I thought it was funny. I was offered dinner dates, shopping trips, weekend breaks. But what was the point? I was here to make money. I'm not stupid, I wasn't going to fall for those tricks.

'The more I said no, the more insistent they became. Soon the language changed. "Let's go shopping" became "Let me look after you", as if I were a child. But their offers weren't accompanied by the keys to a property or a suitcase full of cash. That wasn't what they had in mind. So many words, so few deeds.

'My obstinacy whipped them into frenzy. I loved it. Knowing I couldn't be conquered by conventional means, they devised a new system of seduction

– the subliminal money message, as subtle as a peacock. "My portfolio is up twenty per cent this year" or "Would you like to see my yacht?" My reaction was always to laugh.

'Finally, there came offers of marriage. "I'll look after you" transformed to "I love you". And this from complete strangers! The more I refused, the more love-struck they became. But marriage wasn't for me. I began to wonder how much men thought before pledging undying love. Very little, if you look at the divorce statistics. They just grab for happiness, thrusting themselves forward like dogs mounting one another.

'And what about their inevitable infidelity? Millions of women choose to live in denial, or in a twilight world where they accept it so long as they don't know the details. Or there's the girl married to a man who has become fat and rude, no longer performing his marital duties. Worse if he does – she must lie beneath his heaving carcass until the terrible grunting ends. Now she wears compromise as a badge of honour, works through problems, and fights for love.

'I'm not saying that love and marriage are impossible, it's just that nowadays both start and end so quickly. You say you despair at what you've discovered in space. Surely there's nothing so short-term as human relations?

'Since I wasn't prepared to sell my soul, I decided to rent my body. I played men at their own game. None of them had any intention of making good on their promises. A relationship founded on a trick and fuelled by lust collapses at the first sign of boredom. My father used to say: "Show me a beautiful women, and I'll show you a man who's tired of making love to her." My admirers only wanted one thing, so why not make them pay?

'I choose my clients. I doubt I've been with more boys than Bonnita here. Everything is on my terms, and the rules of engagement are clear. Is that the case with "normal" relations? Also, my price is astronomical. I've made a fortune. I'll go home soon, help my family, and commit to a man, if a good one exists. I've sacrificed something of myself, but I prefer that to a life of almost certain disappointment.'

Tancredi was impressed. This was a spirited tale, delivered with passion. But he was also repelled as much by the slap, which still stung, as her story. Although his upbringing had been complicated, he had been shielded from some of life's harsher truths. Exquisite as she was, he found it hard to empathise with the choices Cocomo had made. He turned towards the angelic Bonnita.

XI

BONNITA'S STORY

I've got no hard luck tale to tell, the opposite in fact. I had a happy childhood, lived in a big house, was spoilt by my parents. I also had the best education. School was a bore, but I was popular because of my looks. Should I be condemned for that? The boys loved me and the girls wanted to be my friend. My teachers thought I was a brat, but I didn't care. I was a cheerleader, my boyfriend was the captain of the football team. We were the golden couple, the prom king and queen.

'The only drag was my father. "You're a smart girl, Bonnita," he'd say. "Find your passion, do something with it. Don't waste your life." One day, I eavesdropped on my parents. My father thought they should cut me loose, otherwise I'd never face the world and make something of myself. Thank God they didn't. It's one of those quirks of nature: parents know they should be tough, but simply can't do it.

'They say when you fall, you fall fast. I fell in record time. I met him at a party. He was in finance, a big hitter – he was perfect. We spent the night together, then the next and the next. My father tried to slow us down, but how do you stop a whirlwind? We were engaged within weeks, married within months. Our wedding was the talk of the town. I was the happiest girl alive! That was the high point.

'It wore off shockingly fast. Polite became inattentive, candlelit dinners turned into "Let's watch TV tonight." A fog descended, then it was downhill all the way – rows, recriminations, rudeness, finally heartbreak and pain. There seems to be a rule that everything ends in a mess. My situation was no different.

'Cocomo ridicules people who grab at happiness, but what's wrong with that? Is love a mathematical equation? Feelings multiplied by time equals love. I was unlucky, but I'm still young. I'll roll with the punches, there'll be another one along some time.

'I keep myself busy. I'm no saint, but I help good causes. It's a question of balance. I do things for others, but I also look after myself. I'd like to find something to be passionate about. Yet nothing stands out. Maybe I'm passionate about leading a normal life. I don't feel the need to achieve anything great, to be challenged or overcome adversity. I never planned to change the world. Can't I just want to be happy?'

Bonnita looked down as she finished her story. Tancredi was about to speak when he noticed a tear gather in the corner of a lovely eye. She was right about love defying logic. He had fallen in a heartbeat. No wonder, she was physical perfection and innocent sweetness combined. He thrilled at the purity of his feelings. He blushed red, not knowing what to say.

He looked about the bar for inspiration, and caught sight of a snout peeping around the open doorway. Kasbek had acquired a sense of the absurd from his new master. He seemed to understand the amusing potential of his pointy proboscis. He was poking it in and out of the doorway by way of announcing his arrival, Tamany in tow. They had exhausted the game of hide-and-seek, and had come to find their travelling companion.

'No young 'uns allowed in the bar,' said the barman.

'Don't worry, he's a grown-up dog,' Tamany shot back.

The barman grunted; he couldn't be bothered to argue.

Cocomo gunned Tancredi with her black eyes; his feelings for Bonnita were obvious.

'So a harlot's no match for an angel?'

She chopped the air with the flat of her hand, as if she was about to give him another slap.

'I thought you were a serious man on a mission to save your world? And yet you fall for a girl who's never carried a single meaningful thought in her head. Is that long-term thinking? I should have hit you harder.'

Tancredi's eyes glazed over, he mumbled something about innocence and beauty which would have certainly activated a CrapOmeter. Bonnita stroked her perfect mane, and wiped away another injured tear. Without warning a hand flew towards Tancredi and connected with his cheek.

'Wake up!' screeched Cocomo.

This time Tancredi did not protest. He was under assault from every direction, not least his own feelings. He nursed his sore face. He knew that he was weak. He could easily lose his mind, pride, money over a girl. When the fire of passion ignited, the feeling of desperation was overwhelming. So often he'd been certain he had met the perfect other who must be possessed, then paraded in public, an exquisite adornment to his being. Now he was sure Bonnita was the one.

Cocomo had observed this affliction at close hand. Tancredi was only its latest victim. Men would do or say anything to conquer a girl. She wished she had recorded all the promises, lies and boasts aimed at her. The embarrassment to her suitors would be excruciating. Men were pathetic. The worst part was the lack of originality in the seduction ritual. Weren't they ashamed of the cliché?

Yet there was something about Tancredi she liked. His statement of purpose – to save the Earth – was absurd, way beyond the boastfulness allowed by the rules of the game. He might even be sincere. Skilled in dealing with the machinations of men, she sensed a naïve honesty she had never encountered before. She decided to persevere a little longer.

'OK, let's explore this,' she said, smiling at her victim.

'The first girl has a perspective on life. She compromises in certain ways, but she has thought things through. She wants to improve her situation, then she'll move on. Most of all, she's true to herself. This girl is rejected.

'The second girl is incapable of a selfless thought – her kindnesses are performed only to salve her conscience. She follows the standard pattern: happiness grabbing, lust, marriage, decline and failure. She doesn't hesitate to break her holy vows. Her reward? The hero sweeps her off to a life of introspective bliss.'

Bonnita thought this explanation too long; it must be masking something. Could Cocomo actually like the hapless young stranger?

'So speaks the whore who epitomises the short-term,' she said. 'Quick coupling for fast money. Must we suffer a lesson in long-term thinking from someone who does hers on her back, staring at the ceiling?'

She moved closer to Tancredi.

'I bet I've spent no more time on my back than you,' Cocomo replied, just a little too angrily, 'and while I was examining the ceiling, you were off on a flight of fantasy about your next wedding. If you'd experienced the divorce ceremony on my moon, you might be a little less eager. In fact, you might lead an altogether less selfish life.'

By now Tancredi was confused beyond words. He couldn't deny his feelings for Bonnita. She might be unaccomplished, but that was part of her charm. But Cocomo was right. Life needed a purpose. Wasn't he on a quest to save humanity, the highest purpose of all?

Bonnita slipped her arm through his, glaring at Cocomo. Tancredi
shuddered to the heart-stopping thrill of being touched by the
most desirable women he had ever seen. The rules of
the game had just been defined. It was the
game of Tancredi, its prize
one and the
same.

XII
TANCREDI GETS DIVORCED

Cocomo had to think quickly. Here was a man who claimed to be enlightened, falling for a flick of the hair and a tear in the eye. Bonnita's victory would be unbearable. She must wake him up. A desperate remedy was required.

She quickly alighted on an idea that was typical of the rigour with which she approached life. In order to wake him, she must first put him to sleep. She unsheathed the stun gun which she used to deal with unruly men, and started blasting.

Tancredi woke in an underground chamber crammed with dinner jackets, all in small sizes. He rubbed his temples: he felt fine but disorientated. He guessed immediately what had happened, though couldn't discern a motive. His query was answered by the bustling figure of Cocomo, who announced: 'We're getting divorced.'

She rifled through the clothing.

'Choose a jacket, hurry up, the ceremony starts soon.'

Tancredi opened his mouth to protest but she was already at the doorway. 'I'm off to get ready.'

Meanwhile, Bonnita, Tamany and Kasbek woke on the floor of a stadium. They were surrounded by a crowd of thousands. Tamany stretched out his little arms and yawned, a gesture copied by Kasbek.

'What happened?' he said. 'Who are all these people?'

'The witch shot us,' Bonnita spat. 'We're on Cocomo's home planet. This is the Eros Two divorce stadium. They're going to perform a ceremony.'

Tamany was about to launch into a series of questions when a whistle sounded.

'Attention, please,' said a sharp voice through loud speakers. 'Everyone link arms.'

'Is it a game?' Tamany asked Bonnita as she threaded her arm through his.

'You'll see,' she replied. 'We'd better do as we're told.'

'Come on, Kasbek, you play too,' he said, raising the confused dog onto his back legs.

The crowd formed into neat lines across the stadium.

Shortly, the tune of 'Who's afraid of the big bad wolf?' blared through the speakers.

The crowd screamed, 'We are!' The ritualistic question and answer was repeated several times.

'You're warmed up,' continued the voice. 'Now, you all know what to do. Start to kick on the count of three. Remember, kick as high as you can.' There was a pause, then the voice shouted: 'One ...two ...three!'

There was a roar from the crowd as they began a synchronised can-can.

'Kick! Kick! Kick!' screeched the voice.

'This is absurd,' Tamany laughed, remembering the Matron on Sanitalis as he kicked his little legs. 'Why is everyone obsessed with this silly dance?'

'No, it makes sense,' replied Bonnita, puffing out her cheeks. 'We all have to practise for when Surprise goes supernova.'

Tancredi felt the vibration of the disaster drill in his subterranean chamber. When he'd refused to co-operate with Cocomo's commands, she'd summoned some guards to help him dress.

'We're not even married,' Tancredi protested.

'Rubbish,' replied a guard, 'no one does the ceremony voluntarily.' He pointed at Cocomo. 'So why would she do this unless you were? Just get dressed.'

Following this altercation, Tancredi was required to squeeze into a dinner jacket several sizes too small. The trousers hung above his ankles and his wrists protruded from short sleeves. He resembled a schoolboy whose parents couldn't afford a new uniform. The outfit was completed by a green, red and yellow fool's cap, featuring multiple peaks tipped by bells.

Cocomo came in, wearing a white taffeta and lace wedding dress with a short hemline that showed off her beautiful legs. Her hands were encased in velvet gloves, her head adorned by a diamond tiara beneath a satin veil. She twirled about with a girlish giggle in front of a mirror. She looked stunning.

'I never thought I'd get divorced before I was married,' she laughed. 'Maybe this is a better way round.'

'Why don't you have to look ridiculous?' Tancredi asked.

'Wait and see,' Cocomo replied.

Another guard, dressed in storm-proof clothing with goggles, arrived in the preparation area.

'You ready?' he clipped.

Cocomo nodded. Tancredi looked vacant.

'Alright then, follow me.'

Tancredi had to be escorted up some stairs to a parking lot beside the arena.

'Don't be such a baby,' said Cocomo, 'we'll do this together.' She grabbed his hand as if he were a child. 'I've always wanted to do it anyway.'

'Please move onto the platform,' a guard said pointing to the back of a vehicle.

As Tancredi climbed up he felt the old fear returning. He despised himself. He wanted to be brave, but he could no more change his character than the colour of his eyes. All he need do was hang on. What was the worst that could happen? A guard tied a roll of cloth onto the back of Cocomo's wedding train, creating a tail of fantastic length. Another ascended the driver's cab and fired the engine.

Then the arena's wrought-iron gates were flung open and the vehicle drove in. As they approached the centre of the arena, the driver pressed a button. The platform on which they were standing rose up into the air, Cocomo's tail dangling beneath. Tancredi began to tap his nose with his free hand. Soon they were parallel with the seated, silent crowd: a beautiful bride beside a groom in a shrunken dinner jacket who was doing something to his nose.

'Today Tancredi and Cocomo are to break the vows they made before God,' the voice announced. 'We're here to remind them to be more thoughtful in the future.'

The vehicle began a circuit of the arena. The platform lurched perilously, oscillating from side to side. Tancredi's hand tightened in Cocomo's. She felt the tension and looked at him.

'What on earth are you doing?' she asked, observing his strange ritual.

Tancredi was too ashamed to answer. Cocomo drew herself up to her full height, held her head up and surveyed the surrounding crowd. She knew she would need all her powers of courage and defiance. She wouldn't succumb like the condemned man who begs forgiveness of his audience. She'd spit at them and laugh.

As the vehicle continued its circuit the crowd got to its feet, all eyes on the couple. Presently the voice announced, 'Point!' Thousands of arms stretched out in silent accusation. 'Laugh!' The crowd convulsed with uncontrollable laughter; not giggles but bellyaching shouts, the guffawing of the madhouse. The laughter rose in pitch and hysteria. Although he hadn't broken any vows, Tancredi felt a terrible shame.

Cocomo stabbed her finger at the crowd. 'Yes you, idiot!' she shouted. 'And you, moron! And you, pathetic!'

The vehicle was driven back to the centre of the arena; the voice sang out again. 'Putrefaction gun!'

A roar of excitement rose from the frantic crowd. Cocomo shouted to Tancredi above the noise: 'Stop doing that thing with your nose. Close your mouth. Shut your eyes.'

The crowd cheered as a salvo of blood and offal arced through the air towards the divorcees.

'Excremortar!' the voice announced to further hoots of enthusiasm.

To his horror, Tancredi couldn't follow Cocomo's advice in time, his finger glued to its olfactory perch. His mouth filled with filth, he gasped for air, but his throat was blocked. He gagged, lent over the platform and was violently sick. This induced a great cheer, which reverberated around the arena like a thunderclap. There followed a chorus of catcalls and boos.

'Who's a messy boy, then?' jeered the voice through the stadium speakers.

The crowd roared the answer.

'Who's a dirty girl who can't keep her wedding dress clean?'

'She is! Her!' screamed the crowd pointing to Cocomo on the platform.

At this point, the voice made an error.

'Who's a bad example to their little boy and doggie?'

The crowd failed to understand the reference and continued to scream insults.

'Stand up,' hissed Cocomo, grabbing Tancredi. Her hand acted like a lightning rod, channelling power to him. He steadied himself on the platform.

'Face them, show you don't care.'

A few minutes later the crowd began to disperse. Tancredi and Cocomo were left on the platform, which was now lowered to the ground. Although Tancredi was shivering with shock beneath his wilted fool's cap, he once again experienced the elation of having survived an ordeal. Cocomo's wedding dress was a mess of splattered blood and excrement. As Tamany and Kasbek clambered onto the platform to comfort their friend, Tancredi scanned the surrounding area for Bonnita. He imagined that she would rush to him and they would embrace. In his mind, his survival of the ceremony was a proof of his love.

Bonnita took her time to pick her way through the grime-filled floor of the arena. When she saw Tancredi, a look of horror spread across her face. She would no more touch him than dive into a vat of dung. Tancredi's hopes of a heroic deliverance melted. It was clear she had no interest in him. Her sole concern was the inconvenience of her abduction.

74

'Animal! Demon! Beast!' Bonnita shrieked, shaking her fist at Cocomo. 'I'll kill you!'

Cocomo attempted to rearrange her muck-ridden hair to comical effect.

'Perhaps you should have a go on the platform. It might focus your mind before your next wedding.'

She threw back her head, laughed, then looked at Tancredi.

'Aren't you going to claim your bride?' she jibed with an expression of mock anguish.

A look of sorrow suffused with stupidity swept his face. The nightmare of the ceremony was nothing compared to the shame he now felt. He deserved his fool's cap. Long-term thinking had been eviscerated by lust, desperation and insecurity. Although Tancredi had temporarily lost his mind, at least he was able to acknowledge the situation he found himself in. The best antidote to heartbreak was a dose of reality. Before him stood the most beautiful girl in the Universe, but one who he realised couldn't care less about him.

Bonnita spotted an opportunity to move her attack from the verbal to the physical. She ascended the driver's cab, soiling her clothes against the grime which clung to its side. She grimaced. It would be worth it. She searched the control panel.

Then she pushed the button marked 'Up'. The platform began to move

skywards. Everyone shouted at her, but to no avail. Soon they

reached the edge of the planet's atmosphere.

Bonnita watched from below as they

were jettisoned into

space.

XIII
SCOOP

Cosmic currents carried the space travellers to a new planet. On entering its atmosphere the rickety platform broke in two, separating Tancredi from the group. He landed on a soft but smelly spot – a rubbish tip. His companions were nowhere to be seen. He presumed they had landed on a different part of the planet – he would have to find them.

Stumbling down the tip, Tancredi looked at his surroundings. This was a strange planet. It appeared to be made of newspapers: paper trees, paper ground, paper walls of a paper building. He was about to set off in search of his friends when a rubbish bag tumbled down the garbage slope, followed by another. Presently the cause of the avalanche was revealed.

A man wearing a little green hat was rootling about the tip making shrill snorting noises. He was sifting through piles of waste with quick nervous gestures, tossing it in every direction like a demented digger. As Tancredi focussed on his face he was surprised to see a flat nose with wide nostrils, large protruding ears and small beady eyes. He appeared to have the DNA of a pig. Oddly, a large pannier was strapped to his backside.

The refuse rifler continued with his labours, ignoring Tancredi.

'Excuse me,' shouted Tancredi, starting to climb back up. 'What planet is this?'

The man-pig looked up with a jolt, and scrutinized Tancredi's face.

'Scoop,' he replied matter-of-factly. Then he bent back to his task, strewing a bag of debris over Tancredi's feet. 'Now buzz off, I'm busy with this rubbish.'

'What are you looking for?'

The man-pig sighed, detached his pannier, and sat down on a pile of newspapers. As his legs twitched with an anxious tic, Tancredi's eyes were drawn to cloven feet.

'A scoop, of course.'

He lent back on his makeshift seat and surveyed the rubbish tip like an emperor. He produced a handkerchief from his trouser pocket and wiped away a bead of sweat with a trotter. A look of weary resignation swept over his porcine face.

'I love a good scoop,' he volunteered, 'but this is a bad news day.'

Tancredi kicked over a discarded crate to make a seat and sat down.

'So what's a good news day?'

The man-pig looked wistful; he seemed to be casting his mind back to ages past.

'I'll always remember when I started,' he snorted. 'I was an apprentice, you know. My editor was a genial chap. He used to say "mek the news yung mun." Then he'd slap me on the back and add, "Politicians, laddy, they're always up to summut."'

Tancredi nodded in encouragement.

'One day I took off to our capital, Read All About It, in search of my first scoop. Arriving at our Parliament, everything was a paradise of propriety. There were strategically placed disabled signs; a notice board containing helpful information starting at A and ending at Z; a warning to coffee machine users to beware of hot water. This was no school for scandal. I put my hands in my pockets and slunk out of the building.'

'I stood on the sidewalk wondering what to do next, looking up at the massive masonry of the façade of government. What secrets lay within, I wondered? What cancer oozed through its marble floors? I decided to go to the back of the building to look for clues.'

'Moving down an alleyway I felt a glimmer of hope. The long arm of health and safety hadn't yet extended to its immediate vicinity. The further down the alley I went, the filthier it became. My nostrils twitched like a pig on the scent of a truffle. At last I arrived at the destination I had anticipated – the

Parliamentary refuse area – the Gomorrah of civic activity.'

He shuddered and cuddled himself with evident pleasure. Trails of saliva appeared to roll down his chin.

'The stench was a combination of mildewed food, mould and vermin shit. Rats scuttled for cover and daylight diminished in protest at the scene. I was indifferent: I neither gagged, nor covered my nose with my hand. I stood in a pool of rancid grey water. The fetid atmosphere could have been lily of the valley for all I cared.'

'I paused for a moment, unsure where to start. My senses were as keen as a whetted knife. I knew that rubbish could contain a golden nugget of information. In amongst the discarded pizzas, rotting food and soiled paper might be something which would enable me to make the news.'

'My search took me into the night. I paused only to buy a torch and a life-sustaining cup of sweet tea from a convenience store. After several hours I discovered a cache of bestial pornography. This was it! The hoard was interspersed with bits of paper which might identify its owner. Might it be a Minister's? But the trail led nowhere. No matter, I continued with my mission.'

'Soon I was working at a frantic pace, oblivious to my surroundings. My clothes became soiled. I resembled the filth I was filtering through my hands. Sometimes, emptying a sack, I sat on the ground amongst its contents to sift its silent story. Bits of debris stuck to my clothes, hands and hair. I didn't care, I was locked in my quest, a missile seeking its target.'

'Dawn was breaking when I made my discovery. Pure radiant light touched the alleyway, illuminating my stinking scattered triumph. I held in my hands a large sealed envelope. My heart began to palpitate. This was it – I felt sure. Who would seal an envelope unless its contents were secret?'

'I ripped it open. A packet the size of a small brick tied with string fell to the ground. As I illuminated it, my torch failed. I held up the package in the dawn light. A bead of sweat fell and smudged a photograph. I swept it clean, which made it worse. I got to my feet. Soon all would be revealed.'

'I made my way back up the alley. Within minutes I settled on the steps of our Parliament. A night watchman glanced at me as he passed. I noticed his disgust. He made a detour to widen the distance between us. Tramps, vagrants, the homeless always end up decorating the steps of our seat of power.'

'I looked down at the package and ran a finger over its surface. With a pull I unfurled the string. The brick was revealed to be a bundle of photographs. The juiciest pictures were of a voluptuous red head beating the naked Minister of Justice with a buggy whip.'

XIV
THE FILTH
FACTORY

Tancredi sighed and ran a hand through his hair in tired defeat. Another planet, another example of self-defeating nihility.

'Rooting through rubbish like a pig,' he said, 'you call that journalism?'

The man-pig examined Tancredi, jerking his head in short, sharp spasms. Suddenly he snorted and leapt off his paper seat.

'I know who you are!' he exclaimed. 'News travels. You're the voyager with the one-size-fits-all philosophy. No wonder you disapprove of a trade which personifies the here and now. But what's wrong with that? News is only news because it's new. You need to re-think your creed.'

'And filth is news?'

'Your pious views are all very well,' the man-pig said, re-taking his seat, 'but since when have pleasantries sold papers? What do people crave – a photo of a sun-filled sky or a bloody battlefield? Nice doesn't sell. You know that.'

He stood up and attached the pannier to his backside.

'People are simple-minded. They want to read about the Neanderthal footballer and his lobotomised wife. Acres of forest are destroyed in the cause of reporting his affairs, her breasts, their nuptials, every sort of vulgarity – the continuing alliance of two great minds in our glorious culture.'

He broke wind into the pannier, unconcerned by his lack of decorum.

'Go on,' said Tancredi.

'And pain, that's a big seller – all the things people want to conceal. Whispered secrets, doleful confessions, bad news, embarrassing results. Fat rolls, sagging skin, varicose veins, unwanted hair, spots, cellulite and wrinkles. People love other people's pain. The misfortune of others is even more satisfying than one's own success.'

He tore a strip of newspaper from his seat and stuffed it into his mouth. Within seconds it had been chewed and swallowed. Tancredi shifted uncomfortably on his makeshift chair.

'Best of all is a combination of mindlessness and pain; anything involving sex, rudeness, embarrassing situations, infantile behaviour and imbecilic opinions. Morons on TV in a house or jungle. So you tell me, who's to blame?'

'Very well,' replied Tancredi looking uneasy, 'but what happens when you go too far?'

'Our readers couldn't care less,' the man-pig shot back. 'You think they don't want their diet of dirt? To be provided with bouncing breasts and beastly breaking news? And what an opportunity for politicians and celebrities, our collaborators in crime, to rise up in righteous indignation. Once they loved us. Now they hate us. What perfect outrage!'

He produced a tablet from an inner pocket and began to type at an urgent pace. Tancredi bent over to look.

'SCOOP! SPACE TRAVELLER FOUND ON RUBBISH TIP!

'From your own reporter ...

'Tancredi, the cosmic scourge of short-termism, has been found barely alive on a rubbish tip.'

'But that's not true,' Tancredi protested, 'I'm fine.'

The man-pig snorted, looking annoyed.

'Oh grow up!' he scolded. 'Since when does the news have to be true?'

Tancredi knew he couldn't win this argument, so he decided to change the subject.

'Can you help me find my friends? We were separated on landing, I've no idea where they are.'

Without warning the man-pig shot off his seat and shook his pannier.

'No problem. They'll be at the Filth Factory. That's where we take all our scoops. My bag's almost full, I'm on my way there now. Come with me.'

Tancredi, perplexed, was about to reply when the man-pig scuttled off the rubbish tip and disappeared down a pathway, pannier flapping behind him. He stood up and followed, struggling to keep up with the man-pig's trotting pace.

Presently, Tancredi caught sight of a giant chimney in the distance attached to a box-shaped building. It belched a dirty-looking yellow smoke. As they approached they were hit by a fierce wind emanating from the factory door. Stray newspaper sheets swirled in the air.

'What's going on?' asked Tancredi.

'That's the Filth Factory where the papers are printed. The presses run hot twenty-four hours a day. They're methane-powered — it's a virtuous circle.' His piggy hand drew a rapid loop in the air. 'We write the news, eat the paper, then produce the gas. No planet in the Universe has such an advanced ecology.'

Suddenly a flying newsheet stuck to Tancredi's face. It read:

'DOUBLE SCOOP! BEAUTY QUEEN LOST IN SPACE!

'From your own reporter ...

'The most beautiful girl in the Universe has crash-landed on the planet, accompanied by a child and a dog. See her photo! Phwoooarh! Look at those tits!'

The man-pig started to hop from one trotter to the other. He brought his hands together with little urgent claps.

'Quick!' he exclaimed. 'A real beauty queen!'

As Tancredi approached the factory doorway, he heard a cacophony of squeaking, shouting and oinking. These coalesced into a single bellowed word: 'Scoop! Scoop! Scoop!' The ground was shaking. The man-pig barged him out of the way and scuttled into the factory without so much as a glance at his interstellar guest.

There was pandemonium inside. Thousands of man-pigs wearing little green hats were stampeding in a circle around a central furnace, into which were being fed methane panniers. Every so often a solitary animal stopped at the edge of the tumult, practised a can-can kick, then re-joined the herd. The incessant clanking of giant printing presses rose above the noise. The combination of charging man-pigs and manic machines created a furious wind, and hundreds of newspaper sheets were whirling through the air.

The cause of the commotion was immediately obvious. Standing to the side of

87

the furnace, three figures were looking around the factory's interior in stunned surprise: Cocomo, Tamany and Kasbek. A phalanx of man-pig photographers with obscene distended camera lenses jostled for position in front of Cocomo. Cries of 'Show us your tits!' echoed in the air. They slathered and snarled, attempting to frustrate each other's work with nasty bites and body butts.

Tancredi had to get to his friends, but the sea of man-beasts was mad with excitement. The most exquisite girl in the Universe had arrived on their planet without warning. This was the scoop to end all scoops.

There was nothing for it. Tancredi took a deep breath and plunged in.

Looking back, he never understood how he navigated the swarm of rampaging creatures. He was jostled like a pinball from one frenzied animal to the next, emerging from the hoggish whirlpool bloodied and bruised, but alive.

'Look! Tancredi look!' shrieked Cocomo, flinging an arm around the battered hero to steady him on his feet. She pointed at the ground. Tiny sparks were flying between porcine feet and the concrete floor. As the stampede intensified, the flashes became bigger and more frequent.

'Any time now,' Tancredi panted, 'the whole factory ...'

He looked about frantically, but there was no escape. They were trapped by the bestial deluge. Tancredi was too dazed to feel fear. In a futile gesture he tried to wrap his arms around his friends. Kasbek whimpered. Tamany and Cocomo stared ahead. Within moments the methane would ignite, and the factory and everyone within would be blown to pieces.

As the countdown to disaster continued, the stampede quickened. Cocomo's beauty seemed to animate the beasts with an inhuman energy. Soon it was impossible to discern snout, trotter or little green hat. All was a colourless blur.

Tancredi squeezed his eyes shut. It felt unmanly to say goodbye, better just to await the end. Suddenly he opened his eyes in shock. He and his fellow travellers were floating in the air. He looked down. The factory floor was receding into the distance. They were caught in a vortex created by the animal stampede, rising slowly towards the factory's glass roof.

'Quick!' shrieked Cocomo, 'link arms and legs!'

The travellers locked their limbs in an aerial embrace, and Tamany flung
an arm around Kasbek. Kaboom! The methane panniers
ignited with an earth-shattering roar. Tancredi
and his companions were blown
through the roof into
the brackish
sky.

XV
THE PINK
PLANET

The methane blast shot the travellers through space onto a pink planet. On landfall, it was difficult to stand upright; the ground had the consistency of a marshmallow. Tamany began a bouncing competition with Kasbek in its corpulent folds. For him, every situation was an opportunity – both for a game and for calm observation. He had also become the curator of items acquired on the expedition. Tancredi now handed him a methane pannier to keep alongside his fool's cap and the Matron's bedpan, his memento from Sanitalis.

Following her ejection from her home planet, Cocomo had had little time for introspection. She only had one gear – forward, normally by way of attack. While she had suffered the divorce ceremony to expose Bonnita's character and win their game, in truth she'd enjoyed it.

In telling her story Cocomo had omitted a detail – she sought conflict. She had even chosen a profession normally fallen into out of desperation as a vehicle for attack. She despised men for their lies and lust and ruthlessly exploited them, an unusual reversal of roles. Extraordinary beauty was a weapon. It could be wielded by conventional means, as demonstrated by Bonnita, or to achieve devastation. Tancredi's new travelling companion could be described in a single word – fighter – but unfortunately she was not one with a sense of balance.

'This is impossible,' she said, falling over. 'It feels warm, and clammy.'

By now Tancredi was accustomed to strange new situations. Landing on a pink marshmallow was no more surprising than coming across an army of the sick, or watching people gorge on pizza in the face of death. They could breath and so survive, wherever they were. Here was another opportunity for revelation.

The travellers stumbled off in search of a clue as to what lay beneath their feet. As they negotiated a bulbous hill, which yielded with every tread, the surface began to undulate. Tancredi put his ear to it.

'There's a rumbling noise underground,' he said. 'We must have landed on a volcano of some sort.'

'I'm not sure,' Cocomo replied. 'Something's wrong.'

It was in her nature to see the negative side of any given situation. Optimism is not an attribute of the huntress. Self-preservation requires a perpetual sniffing for the scent of danger.

They rounded another peak and came upon a rosy cliff face. It towered above them; any progress in that direction was impossible. As they looked up, wondering what to do, the cliff shot upwards. Cocomo herded the group back,

92

shocked at what had been revealed — a gigantic head. At last the enigma was answered. They had landed on the belly of the body attached to the head. The cliff was a hand, which was rubbing sleep from eyes now focussed on them. Kasbek began to bark uncontrollably.

'Steady, Kasbek,' said Tamany, trying to calm his usually compliant steed.

Cocomo threw herself forward; her instinct was to attack, but to what end was unclear. She had no weapons, the enemy was a vast pink mountain, impossible to scale. She managed a few strides forward.

'Where are we?' she demanded, then fell over.

There was a pause, followed by further rumblings. The face rolled back; the travellers were confronted with the rounded foothills of a multiple chin.

'Ooooh! Me tum tum.'

Further rumbles gave way to a loud belch, which enveloped the travellers in a malodorous wind. They shrank backwards. The giant's eyes reappeared above his chin. They contemplated the little group with growing interest.

'Tasty, yum yum?'

None of them knew how to respond to this oblique comment.

'No.' There was a hesitating contemplation, followed by an apparent decision. 'Maybe tasty fun fun?' he tittered, 'yes, fun, fun.'

He clapped his great hands together in evident delight.

Cocomo repeated her question. Her resolve startled the pink giant.

'On Obesitas, of course,' a voice boomed over the mound of his belly, which bounced precariously from the force of his reply. 'I presume you're freaks come to perform in the Show?'

He looked at them quizzically, then giggled and broke into a smile.

'I'm the Game Show Master.'

His face was a pink sea, with great folds of flesh falling like a waterfall beneath his chin. His eyes were miniature emerald beads stuck in the rosy vastness of his fat head. It was difficult to discern their nature – were they inquisitive, clever, mean? His mouth was a cavernous monstrosity; for some reason he had no lips. Tancredi guessed they had been eroded by the constant inward-funnelling of food. He helped Cocomo to her feet, then steadied her.

'We're not freaks, we're humans,' Tancredi said. 'And we know nothing about a show. We're on a quest to save the Universe from destruction.'

Their host was silent, seemingly absorbed in thought. Then he exclaimed: 'Welcome to Obesitas!'

The travellers were almost thrown from his stomach. A huge hand descended from the sky, scooped them off his flesh and deposited them gently on the ground.

'Allow me to assist you with your mission,' he said in a lilting voice.

Tancredi was about to reply when he noticed that the giant was lying on some sort of floating contraption.

'It's a hoverboard,' he explained, seeing Tancredi's look of surprise, 'our means of transport.'

As he spoke, he slipped off the board.

'Unfortunately our bones have dissolved due to our corpulence,' he laughed, regaining his mechanical mount.

Tancredi considered the proposition that this strange new world might contain the answer to his predicament. This species wasn't human; perhaps they'd evolved beyond the petty conceits of mankind.

Cocomo was wary; her experience taught her to beware offers of help. The giant sensed her anxiety.

'Let me put you at ease,' he said. 'I'll tell you about our philosophy of life on Obesitas, then perhaps we can enjoy a Game Show.'

He hovered towards the group, bringing his face close up. It was like being approached by a vast speaking pink blancmange.

'Very well,' Tancredi replied, over a growl of disapproval from Kasbek.

The floating giant flashed a look of disgust at Kasbek, then made himself comfortable, adjusting the folds of his flesh like a blanket.

'Obesitas is an ancient planet,' he began.

'Several millennia ago, our founding fathers considered the basic needs of all living things – food, warmth, sex. Of these, warmth is a given, as our sun shines brightly all year. Sex is important, but there are methods of reproduction that do not involve physical contact between the sexes. They concluded that only food was essential. Our society was therefore founded on the need to eat.'

'But what of other imperatives?' asked Tancredi. 'Friendship, self-esteem, morality?'

'I understand that these attributes are considered important in many societies. But here on Obesitas we keep it simple.' He gurgled his pleasure. 'Everything is boiled down to this single issue. As a result our lives are utterly uncomplicated.'

'But should food dominate a culture?'

'It has at many times on Earth. During the medieval period, being large was considered a sign of prosperity. Only the poor were thin. In the harem of the Turkish Sultan, the more corpulent the female, the greater the favours bestowed upon her. Lovely largeness. Clever people. European artists venerated capacious women as the highest form of beauty. At times corpulence was also linked to erotic arousal – yes! Ah! The sensuous pleasure of food! We have combined these traditions, then distilled them into a simple code for living: food is essential, fat is beautiful; the fatter the better.'

'What about the health risks?' enquired Tancredi.

'Oh, we don't worry about that,' he replied with a chuckle. 'Sanitalis is nearby. They love us, we pander to their every wish. In any event, we're sedentary. We travel on our floating boards, we're never out of breath except when we fall off. As for exercise, we learnt long ago that the battle to stay healthy will always be lost to injury, age or lack of willpower. It's more calming to the mind, which governs health, not to worry about keeping fit.'

'So food is your religion?' asked Tancredi, beginning to understand the logic behind the planet's culture.

The Game Show Master laughed so hard he fell off his board again.

'Goodness me, no!' he exclaimed. 'Of course not. Our society's based on food – isn't our religion obvious?'

Tancredi looked blank.

'Surely you can tell, a child would know the answer,' he said exasperated, then looked at Tamany for help.

'I'm sorry,' replied Tancredi, 'I don't understand. What's the religion of a planet dedicated to food?'

'The Game Show,
of course!'

XVI
TANCREDI'S
LUCKY DIP

The jovial giant flew the group on his hoverboard to the great Game Show Hall of Obesitas, a series of concentric crimson shining bubbles rising into the sky like the effervescence of a foam bath. It towered above the capital city, Lard.

Cocomo was a reluctant passenger; she disliked putting herself in another person's hands. Given that she had no choice, she used the trip to observe the rudimentary operation of the giant's machine. Tancredi was focussed on the remarkable new planet they were experiencing. He was amazed by the religion on Obesitas, and said as much to his pink host.

'Consider this,' the Game Show Master replied. 'You worship at church on Sunday morning. We worship before the television on Saturday night. You devour Christ's body and blood. We eat pizza and drink beer. But your world is irreligious. On Obesitas, the entire planet is dedicated to the Game Show. I don't wish to be disparaging, but our Game Show is far more important to our people than your God is to yours.'

'But what about Government?'

'Politicians in other worlds fawn on the people. They shape their speeches, seeking to draw people in with words like "change", "trust", "fairness". And the result? People don't believe them, and couldn't care less. Governments come and go, lurching from one expedient to the next.'

He paused, weighing up the importance of what he was about to say.

'We Game Show Hosts realise a simple truth – the people are morons. That's how to treat them. They are moved by the lowest common denominator. The more mindless, the better. Serve up infantile questions and idiotic tasks. Turn unmarried mothers and hard-luck delinquents into heroes. Give them a focus. Give them hope.'

He gurgled and licked the area around his mouth.

'This is where the power lies, this is what matters.'

'So treating people like Neanderthals is enlightened?' asked Tancredi.

'Imagine the reaction if politicians in other worlds were to announce, "You're all idiots, you'd better watch TV all day." They can't, so they dissemble and use weasel words. They pose like actors playing silly cameo roles to show how much they care. We, on the other hand, have the strength to speak the truth. One day the whole Universe will be ruled by Game Show Hosts.'

'And you mistook us for freaks come to play in a show?' Tancredi said.

'Forgive me. We have a prurient interest in our contestants, of course. You're so different, you'd be a great success. I meant no offence. You should play. All visitors to our world do.'

'No thank you,' Cocomo cut in.

Something about the planet and its pink ruler disturbed her; she couldn't tell exactly what. She wondered how difficult it would be to hijack a hoverboard and spirit themselves off the planet. Following his recent divorce, Tancredi was also wary about subjecting himself to another cultural experience in an alien world. The Game Show Master sensed that Tancredi was unconvinced.

'Bad sport!' he said with a laugh. 'Not going to play! Very well, if you won't, at least be my guest for a game of lucky dip. It's fun! It's funety-tumpety tum-tum it is!'

He squealed with pleasure.

Moments later, as their host hummed what sounded like an advertising jingle, they passed through the entrance of the bulbous Game Show Hall, the centre of the planet's activities. The hall was like a cathedral, but instead of seats there were rows of docking stations for the hoverboards. Each row was separated from the next by a giant conveyor belt, snaking around the hall. This carried a series of pipes which resembled a cross between a praying-mantis and an old-fashioned petrol fuel pump.

As the conveyor belt passed a recumbent board rider, the mantis device bent down and directed a tube into the open waiting mouth. It shuddered, then the recipient's cheeks expanded as a creamy goo gushed into the proffered orifice. The mantis then bent low over the face, and wiped away any spilt slime that had slithered into the folds of the obese faces. The hall reverberated with hoots of pleasure as the rotund gluttons rolled around their mats after a feeding.

Tancredi noticed that each mantis had a sign which advertised the type of feast on offer. Names like Mighty Burger, Macro Potato and Bustin' Bobbins Cherry Glupe enabled eaters to select their favourite feast. Each cheered as a fleshy hand was raised to arrest the feeding fountain; once filled they gurgled and hooted their sated pleasure. The hall rang with a gluttonous porcine noise; there were thousands of them present. The Game Show Master tooted a jovial burble as he entered to attract the feeders' attention. His voice was picked up by a microphone which broadcast his greeting to the audience.

They moved to the centre of the hall, and arrived at a door embossed with a question mark, its period point in the shape of the letter 'O'.

'Here's where we play,' the Game Show Master giggled. 'Have a go, we'll wait outside.'

As Tancredi dismounted, his host handed him a torch and a pink cloak emblazoned with the same stylised question mark.

'Lucky dip is played in the dark,' he tittered, 'it's more fun that way. And this is a luminous Obesitas Game Show cloak for you.'

'Can I play?' said Tamany, trying to shush Kasbek's incessant growls.

The Game Show Master shot the dog another disquieting look.

'Unfortunately you wouldn't be able to reach,' he replied, his eyes twinkling.

'I don't think anyone should play,' Cocomo cut in, 'we're not the sporty types.'

The Game Show Master's face furrowed in disappointment; he looked as if he was about to cry. Tancredi thought that etiquette required some show of enthusiasm.

'Are there any rules?' he asked.

'None. That's the beauty of it. We don't even need to think to have fun!'

He licked the area around his mouth that would usually be reserved for lips.

'Just dip into the barrel. Oh yes! Dip. Dip away my dear!'

Having survived the *Invincible*, Sanitalis, Eros Two and Scoop, Tancredi felt bolder than the uncertain youth of only a few days before. There was no longer a knot of fear in his stomach. Could it be that he had found courage? Beyond this, he was aware of another sensation. Bonnita had been a false start. His feelings for her hadn't emboldened him when blasted by the putrefaction gun or the excremortar.

With Cocomo it was different, he felt a better man. He had never imagined someone could be so defiant in the face of adversity. He was inspired by it. On Earth, the religion of short-termism required everything to be analysed through the prism of one's own self-interest. The result was a sort of predictable, mendacious mediocrity. Cocomo faced the world armed with her beliefs; to hell with what people thought.

And yet he was a weakling compared to her. As the Game Show Master sniggered and burbled awaiting his response, Tancredi saw an opportunity to demonstrate the blossoming of his independent spirit. He had read about chivalric love in medieval times, where the knight performs a task to prove his bravery and win the love of his lady. A game of lucky dip could hardly be compared to slaying a dragon. Nevertheless, there was something daunting about the door emblazoned with a question mark before him. Cocomo's insistence that he shouldn't play was a further spur.

He relieved the great hand of the cloak and put it on. The Game Show Master hooted at his audience with a high-pitched gurgle akin to clearing his throat.

'We have a playooor! We're going on a trip to the lucky dip dip,' he crooned.

Tancredi took hold of the torch and, for no apparent reason, turned in a circle with his arm raised. He was appalled by himself. He had fallen into being a contestant. The Game Show Master produced a whistle, concealed in the folds of his flesh. He blew on it, making a mewing dissonance of noise which attracted the complete attention of the audience.

'Let the show commence!' he fluted and blew his whistle again.

The audience responded by shouting what sounded to Tancredi like, 'Wee humpy, humpy boom boom, croc croc munsi!'

As the heavy door opened light on its hinges, a klaxon brayed the commencement of activity to the slobbering audience. Tancredi trained his torch into the interior gloom. The lucky dip barrels, the height of a man and twice as wide, were lined up in a circle around the chamber. Each barrel was accessed by a step ladder. As he entered the room, Tancredi noticed the red flicker of infrared cameras following his every move. The door shut behind him.

He felt awkward to be the subject of a television show, but at least there wasn't an audience pelting him with excrement here. Although muffled, he could hear the whoops of the crowd outside. There seemed to be applause and some shouting, as well as laughing. He could hear the Game Show Master's voice over a speaker, but couldn't understand what he was saying. The audience were screaming 'Croc munsi!' repeatedly in time to the blast of his whistle.

Tancredi moved to the first barrel, mounted the steps, and swung his arm over the edge. There was a crescendo of excitement from outside, frenzied cries of 'Croc munsi!' rang in the air, but he found nothing inside the barrel. He heard what he thought was crying from the collective masses, then the calming voice of the Game Show Master interceding as he moved on.

He could again hear him winding up the audience as he approached the next barrel. An electric organ thrummed a series of chords that rose with the screams of the crowd as he ascended the steps to the barrel. Again, it was empty. Once more there were groans of disappointment from outside. He examined the next few barrels, nothing, just inky blackness. Each time he approached and leaned over a barrel he heard the same cries of anticipation, then anti-climactic groans and the mollifying interjection of the Game Show Master.

Tancredi began to suspect that maybe this was an elaborate joke. He guessed his viewers knew what his reward would be. He stopped to rest his torch arm over the edge of a barrel when he heard a thrashing sound below. He thought he could hear screams of hysteria outside, there was an incessant howl of 'Muns! Muns! Muns!' A white hot pain shot up his arm, then darkness descended.

All the outside noise evaporated, Tancredi screamed the scream of a man falling to certain death. It seemed the world was howling with him. He clutched his arm, fell backwards off the step ladder and hit his head on the floor. He was conscious of the crowd whooping outside. Unable to stand, he crawled on one side using his free arm for propulsion, quite where he had no idea. He bumped up against a barrel, immediately the thrashing started again. Tancredi squirmed backwards in horror, crying out in panic as well as pain.

He began to feel faint; his arm was gushing blood from a diminishing well. He again became conscious of sounds from outside the room, more hooting and shouts of 'Munch! Munch! Munch!' Then he heard the Game Show Master shout:

'Jackpot One! Jackpot Number One!'

He knew this wasn't for his benefit. He touched his wound. Something hideous had happened. He tore off his pink cloak and wrapped it around his arm, the flow of blood extinguishing its luminescence. Tancredi realised that the only means of escape was the door through which he had entered.

He groped his way along the line of barrels hoping to find it, but it was taking too long. A wave of nausea curled up from nowhere and shook him. The Game Show Master's whistle had been replaced by the regular thump of a bass drum. He retched, convulsions racked his body. Dizzying lightness descended as he heard the groan of voices outside.

A thought occurred to him, as warming as his blood. If this was the end at least it would be over soon. The thrashing sounded again in the dark. The thought vanished, replaced by an image of his tombstone: 'Tancredi, failure, killed playing lucky dip in the dark'. He had no more energy for an escape. The best he could do was compose himself and wait for the end. He closed his eyes and fell sideways in a half-faint, catching himself against a metal object – the door handle.

Tancredi focussed on counting down from ten in an attempt to prolong his last moments. He maintained a momentum up to six. At five he faltered, four and three came out of nowhere, two was a terrible strain. As he reached one a strange force took hold of him, punching through his delirium. He grasped the door handle. It opened and he fainted into the Game Show Hall, unaware of the cries of adulation ringing out across the planet in his honour.

Tancredi awoke the next day in a white room, with a nurse on a hoverboard by his bedside.

'You've lost a lot of blood,' she said, 'you're lucky to be alive.'

Tancredi looked at the stump of his right arm cut off below the elbow.

'I saw it happen,' she continued, 'it was fun!'

She hummed the Game Show theme tune, then hovered closer to her patient as if searching for the missing limb. Tancredi stared at her blankly, his incomprehension plain.

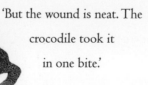

'But the wound is neat. The crocodile took it in one bite.'

XVII
THE END
GAME

Such was the demand for Tancredi following his heroic exploit that he was given only hours to recover from his injury. The show had to go on. Shocked, sickened and white with loss of blood, he once again stood before a Game Show congregation – this time wrapped in his gore-stained cloak. He had no time to mourn the loss of his limb; this was the least of his worries. How could he have been so naïve? A people dedicated to food and obsessed with game shows was the definition of hell. He now expected the worst.

Beyond this he felt an overwhelming stupidity. Every character trait he had exhibited – fear on the *Invincible*, cowardice on Sanitalis, love on Eros Two, bravery on Scoop and Obesitas – was united by a common thread ... idiocy. He knew that his instincts were right. The Universe could only be saved by long-term thinking. He understood the theory, but hadn't mastered the practice. Having gained a little confidence, he'd plunged headfirst into an abyss.

A crowd of thousands, each randomly falling off their machines, was gathered in the great Game Show Hall. Tancredi stood on a stage in the middle. A praying mantis device passed on a conveyor belt nearby. It raised its head, flicking various brightly coloured tubes in his direction, and offered him a dessert featuring a dizzying array of ingredients. Tancredi felt no fear. He wondered if this was what happened to people after so much hardship. A survival instinct kicked in, the sufferer became inured to adversity.

He looked across the hall of bobbing heads and bodies and spotted Cocomo and Tamany on another stage nearby, guarded by two hoverboard riders. They looked horrified. Tears rolled down Tamany's cheeks; he was held in a close grip by Cocomo, whose head was darting in every direction searching for escape. Momentarily, Tancredi saw the cause of their dismay. To the side of the stage was a pyre of kindling wood over which Kasbek was suspended on a spit. A terrible dog scream, pitiful to hear, echoed through the hall. Tancredi recoiled in shock; this was beyond nightmare.

An organ parped a few jittery notes of excitement, the beaming Game Show Master hovered into the hall. He had done this a thousand times. He looked happy and relaxed, acknowledging the cheers of the crowd with a wave of his meaty hand.

'Tonight's show features our one-armed hero,' he announced, without a trace of remorse.

He turned and beamed at Tancredi.

'It's called: "Can the Earthling save his friends?"'

A roar of approval echoed through the hall, and great arcs of goo flew into the air as some joining the tumult regurgitated their food.

'We start with an easy question.'

The Game Show Master looked about the hall. His flock was rapt with attention. He raised a hand, the electric organ gave three brief trills. Silence followed.

'Our guest comes from a planet with a nearby moon.'

There was a pause to allow his audience to absorb this information, followed by a blast from the organ's trumpet key.

'It's believed that small traces of cheese have been found in the moon rock – probably emmental, but scientists can't be sure. The question is ...' As he paused for effect, the organ quivered a rising note.

'... is the moon made of cheese?'

Tancredi exhaled, his brow furrowed in concentration. Whatever terrors he faced, he had to get this right. The audience participated by giving conflicting advice, all of a culinary nature. Tancredi turned to the Game Show Master, who raised his hand. Once again they were surrounded by silence.

'And little Earthling, the answer is?'

'The moon is made of metallic iron with small amounts of nickel and sulphur. Its core is partly molten.'

There was a cascading series of discordant notes on the organ.

'I'm sorry, that's the wrong answer.'

His host sounded disappointed. There were 'ahhs' of sympathy from around the hall.

'We know that the moon is, in fact, made of cheese.'

The organ came alive with a thrilling cascade of tremeloed chords. The Game Show Master nodded to an attendant, who lit the kindling.

'Better luck next time,' he said as the wood began to smoke.

'For the love of God!' Tancredi shouted, leaping forward.

He was intercepted by a hoverboard rider, the organ sounding a note of distress as the pink mountains of flesh rolled around in excitement. Some cried, others made a hideous suction noise with their mouths.

'Our guest was recently on Sanitalis,' continued the Game Show Master.

A murmur of interest arose from the congregation.

'Which of the following is true? A. The State shouldn't care for the obese: they're responsible for their condition. B. The State should care for the obese, irrespective of cost. C. The State should care for the obese and compensate them: it is at fault for creating the conditions under which people are unable to control their eating.'

Tancredi now understood the rules of the game and answered 'C.'

'Bravo!' exclaimed the Game Show Master, as the organ sounded a merry chord sequence. The crowd cheered as one being. The kindling began to catch, engulfing Kasbek in smoke. A disembodied yelp rang from the pyre.

'Kasbek!' screamed Tamany, writhing in Cocomo's grasp. Her heart melted for him, but now wasn't the time for a rescue attempt.

'I gave the right answer,' pleaded Tancredi, 'free Kasbek.'

'That's not how it works,' the Game Show Master laughed, glancing in the direction of Cocomo and Tamany.

The message was clear. Kasbek was lost. If he gave another wrong answer, the others would follow. The organ parped a series of discordant notes at incredible volume.

'The star Surprise will shortly go supernova. It threatens to destroy the Universe. Will we be saved if all the inhabitants of every world join in a synchronised can-can?'

At the mention of the dance, Tancredi kicked out a leg in rage and despair. A hoverboard rider nearby tried to imitate the Game Show hero. Instantly he fell off his machine. Tancredi kicked again, another copied him and fell.

'Look at me! Look at me!' screamed Cocomo, jumping up and down, waving her arms.

Thousands of beady eyes focussed on her. She began to hop from one leg to the other with incredible dexterity.

'They're morons, Tancredi,' she shouted as she danced. 'Dance! Kick!'

He opened his mouth as if he didn't understand, then nodded. Although unbalanced by the loss of his arm, he started to kick as high and hard as any chorus-line dancer, his face a picture of concentration. He had good reason, he was kicking for his life.

The hoverboard rider guarding Cocomo attempted the step. 'Urgh! Urgh! Urgh!' he wheezed. Seconds later, he too slipped off his machine. Another tried to kick whilst being fed by a mantis device, disturbing its smooth operation. Enraged, the machine beat him about the head. The conveyor belt juddered to a stop. This confused the feeding devices, and great arcs of goo flew through the air like fireworks. As the kicking craze spread across the hall, the organ parped a series of shanty-like cadences, whipping the congregation into an ever-more urgent can-can. Hoverboards clashed, and goo-covered pink limbs twisted as riders collapsed in a sea of Obesian flesh.

Cocomo seized her chance. She picked up Tamany and raced over to Kasbek. As soon as he had been liberated, they leapt onto a vacant hoverboard and sped towards Tancredi.

'Stop them!' screamed the Game Show Master.

Blubbery arms lashed out, then lost their target as Tancredi vaulted onto the contraption.

'Kill them! Switch them off!' echoed across the hall, but it was too late for the layered rolls of flesh to react.

The hoverboard sped towards the exit. As they approached they saw two guards wearing little blue caps. They struggled to disengage from their feeding machines and align their mats to intercept them. Covered in goo, they collided with each other as the hoverboard tore its way to freedom.

XVIII
CORRECTOMONDO

Tancredi was bitterly cold. He tried to stand up, but found himself falling into crisp, crunching whiteness. It dawned on him that he was entombed in snow. Great flakes brushed his eyelids to confirm the fact.

He remembered the hoverboard spinning out of control. Cocomo had been operating the machine, it wasn't difficult to pilot. Suddenly it felt as if it had been hijacked by an alien force, which then guided it to this frigid landscape. He was thrown as it crashed.

How long had he been unconscious? Where were his friends? He tried to nurse the stump of his arm, but his hand was frozen and he had no feeling in his feet. At least the cold anaesthetised the pain of his wound.

The horror of his amputation struck him for the first time. Part of him had been eaten. He felt sick. He was disabled, a freak, and all for the amusement of a planet of immobile gluttonous morons. Soon, no doubt, reality TV on Earth would feature contestants being dismembered in the dark by reptiles.

At the same time, he felt an odd sense of pride. How many people could say they had survived an encounter with a man-eater? Stumps and scars were only unsightly to others. His lost arm was a visible badge, one which would be recognised by Cocomo in whose honour it had been won. As he rested, the ice-cold snow numbing his stump, he started to wonder how Cocomo would view his valour. He feared she might take a more realistic view of his endeavour.

He thrust his good arm into the snow to see if he could find the ground. It sank to his elbow.

The silence was total, not even a whisper of a breeze. He looked around the field, then took a few steps, testing his ability to negotiate the snow. He knew he needed to find shelter fast. A thought which calculated his survival in minutes, not hours, was quickly dismissed.

As he stumbled forwards, shaking with shock, squinting against the blistering cold, he saw a figure running towards him. After his experience on Obesitas, he considered trying to escape – but where would he go? Anyway, he was too weak to flee.

The runner came panting up, vapour billowing from his mouth. He wore a coat made of plaid bulked out with numerous layers, and an ushanka with flaps like great dog ears. He had been running in knee-high fur boots, heavy footwear even at a walking pace. Thick fur gloves covered his hands. He stopped in front of Tancredi and bent over to catch his breath.

'Thank God I found you,' he gasped. 'Come, quickly.'

Tancredi looked into a thin face with a beard greying at the edges. His eyes were mere slits surrounded by frosted eyelashes and brows. He grabbed Tancredi's arm and pulled him forwards through the white drift. After a few steps, Tancredi saw a flicker of light; there was a house in the distance. Time slowed. Suddenly he was inside, shivering uncontrollably. His rescuer laid him out by a fire, threw off his gloves and began to massage Tancredi's limbs, restoring him to life. Within moments, Cocomo and Tamany were by his side.

As Cocomo lost control of the hoverboard, Tancredi had tried to steady himself, but become unbalanced. She had seen him slip off the edge of the craft. Horrified, she had prepared herself for the worst. Now she looked down at the figure by the fire, and experienced an odd new sensation. Since men were the enemy, she was surprised by the thoughts playing in her mind. Tancredi had taken part in the game on Obesitas for her benefit. Silly boy, as if she cared. Still, men had only ever offered her lies, boasts and false promises, all to a squalid end. No man had ever attempted a heroic act in her honour.

That Tancredi was weak had been clear when she first met him, but she knew this wasn't due to lust, greed or dishonesty, the triumvirate of exclusively male diseases. He was just naïve, which was almost attractive. Callow youth! He had a sort of childlike integrity; no wonder he was friends with Tamany. She also believed in his stated purpose, no matter how absurd it sounded. What all this added up to, she couldn't say. Like most people who have been hardened by life, Cocomo's tough exterior concealed something softer within. The new sensation which surprised her so much emanated from this inner core.

Tamany had been panic-stricken to see Tancredi fall, and was about to follow him over the edge when Kasbek grabbed hold of his leg. Tamany now danced about the fire, crowing that he had known that Tancredi would survive the fall. In truth, the alternative was too shocking to contemplate.

After losing his parents, Tamany had thought about which was better – orphanhood or being raised by appalling parents? He felt it must be the former. At least now he could face the world unencumbered by people who should love him, but didn't. The moment he had found Tancredi on the deck of the *Invincible*, he knew they would be a family.

Later, the group sat by a fire, Kasbek at their feet licking a sorry-looking singed tail. Tancredi's rescuer gave him a steaming bowl of broth.

'I must start with an apology,' he said. 'I brought you here.'

He tossed a log onto the fire.

'I took control of your craft, and chose this wilderness as a landing spot. You must have been thrown as you descended, but your friends were rescued.'

Tancredi closed his eyes in evident despair. Here was another stranger, another fake proposition to encounter. What would happen this time? Would his captor turn into a monster? Practise an inventive snow torture on him?

'Let me speak, then you can judge,' said his host, judging his reaction.

Cocomo had already heard his story.

'Listen to him,' she said.

A commendation from Cocomo was rare. Tancredi opened his eyes and studied the little man. Freed from his storm-proof clothing, he was dressed in a shabby tweed suit. Long hair flew randomly around a face whose tired eyes betrayed years of disappointment. His delicate features were those of an aesthete who had suffered for his art, his political beliefs or both.

'You're on Correctomondo,' he began, 'a planet dedicated to political correctness.'

Tancredi didn't know whether to laugh or cry. Correctomondo! Whatever next?

'I'm a dissident professor – I need your help.'

His eyes fixed on Tancredi, trying to create rapport.

'You kidnap me and expect co-operation?'

'On Correctomondo,' replied the Professor, ignoring the question, 'to refer to a woman as a woman is not permitted. It's considered sexist.'

He brought a silencing finger to his lips.

'Instead they are called "not men".'

He smiled wearily at Tancredi, hoping he had fired some kind of interest.

'For years, the planet has been governed by the Middle Way party. They are now being challenged by the Centre Way party. In clinging to office, the ruling party is implementing a programme of total political correctness. This will finally destroy us.'

'What's this got to do with me?' asked Tancredi, warming himself by the fire.

He had escaped Earth to find a solution to its predicament, not to become involved in the politics of a far-away world.

'Word of your exploits has spread. It's said you champion thoughtfulness in a universe obsessed with the fast and simple. Correctomondo is idiocy personified.'

'Why has your world become like this?'

The Professor had rehearsed the answer a thousand times.

'Over time, changes in science, technology and welfare have transformed our planet. As a result the populace are lazier, ruder and less thinking than at any period in our history. They take their new privileges for granted, cling to entitlements, are quick to resort to the law. To slip on the pavement is a positive, because the authorities can be sued.'

'The effect on our politics has been devastating. Politicians no longer propose radical solutions to difficult problems for fear of causing offence. Every word they utter is calculated, every policy focus-grouped to death. Our leaders are now judged on who can appear the most reasonable, caring and correct. Facing reality and doing the right thing are considered negative. Power is based on who can occupy the middle ground.'

This didn't make sense to Tancredi. Reason existed in consensual debate and shared thought.

'But what's wrong with the middle?' he asked.

'Middle is just another word for mediocre. We live in a world where respect and discipline have collapsed because they're viewed as extreme. Crime is on the increase, law-breaking amongst youngsters out of control. The streets are no longer safe. The solution's obvious – compulsory National Service. Imagine if a politician were to suggest this. He'd be branded a fascist.'

The old thinker spat out these words with deliberate sarcasm.

'And then there's immigration. Millions come illegally, live off our planet, cause untold trouble. Again, the answer's obvious – round them up, send them away, stop new arrivals. What do we do? Create an ever-more complex structure of laws and appeals to protect their human rights.'

'So what can I do to help?'

The Professor walked over to Tancredi, knelt down, and brought his face close.

'You must cause a revolution,' he said passionately. 'You claim to be a long-term thinker. In today's world, that's another word for revolutionary. This is what we need. Rupture, reform and change are only clichés in the mouths of politicians. They're unable to act because to do so would defy our Correctomondo mores.'

His hands became animated and a slender finger poked at Tancredi.

'You say that since death is inevitable, we should all try to make a difference in life. You can, here on this planet.'

Tancredi brought a hand to his forehead and slumped back in his chair. The Professor stood up and started to pace in front of the fire, discouraged by Tancredi's lack of response.

'At least observe our Leader at close hand. Then decide.'

His eyes strayed to the far side of the room, out of Tancredi's line of sight.

'There is, however, a small problem to overcome.'

Tancredi followed his gaze. He had been so focussed on the conversation he

hadn't noticed a figure slumped in the corner wearing an overcoat.

He stood up and walked over to introduce himself. As he

approached, the figure looked up from beneath

a military cap with the Star of Lenin

on its peak. Tancredi flushed

red. The man seated

before him was

Joseph

Stalin.

XIX
THE MIDDLE
WAY

As Tancredi recovered from the shock of meeting one of the most notorious dictators in history, the Professor finished his story.

'While I was capturing your craft, a foreign object bisected the energy beam that was drawing you in. It turned out that Stalin had discovered a method to travel in time and space. Unfortunately he was caught in the beam and brought to Correctomondo with you.'

'Unfortunately?' interrupted the Russian dictator.

He stood up and shuffled towards the Professor.

'You seek a long-term thinker? Someone to bang heads together? To start a riot? Here I am!'

The Russian beamed at the little group with smug satisfaction and slapped his gloved hands on his knees.

Joseph Stalin, General Secretary of the Communist Party, was exactly as Tancredi had seen him in photographs. His pallid white face was dominated by a large moustache and quizzical dark eyebrows. Pale grey eyes narrowed into menacing beads as they focussed. He was shorter than Tancredi would have expected – but pictures rarely conveyed a sense of height. His shoulders were broad and his coat made him look square. Tufts of thick grey hair escaped from beneath his cap.

Tancredi was incredulous. Of all the situations he'd encountered on his voyage, the idea that he should ferment a revolution with a famous killer was the most farcical. While he declined the invitation, he agreed to attend a speech the Leader was giving, as much out of curiosity as anything else. In return, the Professor undertook to adapt his energy beam to power a rocket on which they could escape the planet. Cocomo remained behind to supervise the construction of their means of escape.

Tancredi found himself tucked beneath a blanket with Stalin, who took up three-quarters of the bench, on the back of a sledge. It was snowing lightly under a crystal blue sky. The sledge set off at a walking pace down a track covered in snow. Tancredi waved goodbye, and Tamany and Kasbek ran off to play. As the sledge reached a bend in the track, Tancredi took a final look back. Cocomo was standing in the snowdrift, her arm raised, seemingly oblivious to the cold.

A few hours later, Tancredi and Stalin arrived at the headquarters of the Middle Way party. Tancredi was sore and not a little annoyed with his travelling companion, who had been unsatisfied with the amount of space he had allotted to himself. Tancredi had struggled to avoid being forced to ride on the sleigh's runners.

The Professor had arranged for them to attend a rally of the party faithful where the Leader would speak. They entered an auditorium and found seats at the front. After a while, a gentle note sounded and the Leader appeared, dressed in a saffron-coloured robe which failed to conceal the plump curvature of a well-rounded stomach. He had a long walk from the side of the stage to the lectern, one designed to give the audience plenty of time to admire their leader. It also allowed Tancredi the opportunity to study him.

He was a short man with a bird-like face, who gave off an aura of prudish precision. He walked with a measured pace, his hands held together at chest height like a priest parading into church. He wore a fixed smile and, at regular intervals, studiously inclined his face to the audience, nodding to acknowledge their cheers. The impression was of a fat cat walking along a narrow fence, tail in the air. Stalin collapsed with laughter.

The Leader of the Middle Way party believed himself to be good. He thought about others and wished to make things better. He sometimes dreamt of ascending skywards, arms outstretched, stomach held in, bathed in light. His lower lip quivered as he rose, and the chime of a shinto gong rang out. 'All is well, all is well, all is well. You are the true guide. Lead them, Leader. They will follow.'

But it had not always been so. As he ascended the podium he cast his mind back to the early days of his political career. An insignificant official in local government, he had struggled to gain a foothold on the ladder of political correctness. One night he shed tears of desolation, wherein lay his salvation.

'Shared tears' was his brainchild. A programme of job selection, it stated that society's true customer was the one who had the least. The policy required dominant caste members to cry openly with people from minority backgrounds, and, in the process of shedding tears, to give up their positions in society for the benefit of minorities.

Following this, the young zealot conjured an idea of even greater political rectitude – the mandatory foreign guest day. This compelled everyone on the planet to dress once a year in an immigrant costume of their choice, and speak and behave like members of that ethnic group for a day. People already wore costumes for Hallowe'en and fancy dress parties. The entire planet could now dress for a purpose, to learn and share as one. The policy was impossible to oppose. Imagine the rebuke to a dissenting voice. The mandatory foreign guest day became the physical manifestation of the dream of total equality. A great political career was born.

His eyes swept the audience; the Leader understood the laws of speechifying. Years of experience had taught him to build dramatic tension by looking beyond the crowd, the great man seeking the far horizon. Stalin also understood the art. Only novices could not contain their nerves and started speaking too soon. Tancredi leant forward; Stalin sat hunched in his great coat, arms crossed.

'Brothers,' he began in a reassuring voice, 'the Centre Way party seeks to steal the great and caring mantle of centrality from us.'

He nodded as if to confirm this prognosis.

'We must therefore double our efforts to tread this path with that responsibility of purpose which only our Party can carry.'

The audience murmured their agreement.

'Today,' he paused and allowed his voice to echo back to him, 'I unveil our new manifesto – "At One Together!"'

He smiled his smile of confidence.

'What?' shouted Stalin.

The audience stirred, the Leader looked down in surprise at his heckler. This was unprecedented; never before had a speech on Correctomondo been interrupted.

'Sound bite, cliché,' spat Stalin. 'Meaningless notice on a closed door. What does "at one together" mean?'

Tancredi put his hand on the dictator's arm, trying to calm him.

'I'd like to begin with sports,' said the Leader, ignoring the brutish disruption, 'which are always popular with our people.' He held out his arms gathering the audience in, then frowned to indicate a change of mood.

He remembered his own sporting career. He had been the fat boy at school, with a round face and square body who always finished last. Once he had been obliged to compete in a hurdle race. He puffed up to the first jump, but was unable to get airborne. His schoolmates roared with laughter as he kicked out a fat leg, toppled the hurdle, then skipped over it like a girl. His parents were unable to meet his eye at the finish line. Now he would put everything right.

'For too long, sports have favoured the spectacle of the able-bodied over the handicapped, an unequal condition.'

His eyes swept the audience, seeking its approval. Although ignorant of the policy he was about to announce, his flock bleated their agreement to what was obviously correct.

'Sports today are for shiny-toothed heroes, chisel-cheeked with tousled hair and all their limbs. I applaud the paralympics and facilities for the disabled at sporting events around Correctomondo. No run through a city is without its amputees using prosthetic legs, and competitors in wheelchairs. But the question is this: have we gone far enough?'

Like the statesmen that he was, the Leader's voice became firmer as he spoke.

'In future, sports will be restricted to the disabled.'

There was an audible murmur from around the hall as members of the audience looked at one another to check that this was indeed a brilliant idea. The Leader smiled a smile of omniscience.

'For example, only amputees using prosthetic legs will participate in marathons, although there will be an exception for wheelchairs. This will also cause a revolution in the science of prosthetic materials.'

The audience recognised the inspirational insight of the new policy and greeted it with warm applause.

A strong Russian voice rang out from the front row: 'Madness! Utter madness!'

Although omnipotent, the Leader didn't know what to do. He shot a worried glance at the uninvited guest before battling on.

'Education is dear to all our hearts.'

He held his hands to his chest. His audience were with him, he could afford a dramatic pause in which to reflect on his own education. He had wanted to excel but was not a natural student. Everything had to be memorised. Although this was obviously a good method for learning, he had led a student revolt against it. Looking back, he couldn't remember whether he had done this out of conviction, or as a way to stand out.

'Learning things by heart isn't education but a memory test. This is no way to shape the minds of children or early learning developers, ELDs for short, as I prefer to call them.'

He smiled at the modernity of the description: a new buzzword to play with, another way to parry the silly questions of the controversial interviewer.

'Teachers imposing views on ELDs is out-dated. It stifles individual initiative. Knowledge is a collective human experience gained by exploration. The internet provides a wealth of information. ELDs are far more adept than their teachers at using it.'

'I believe ELDs should be allowed to roam free, to explore, to experiment and discover new areas and subjects. Teachers should act as facilitators, or crowd controllers if you like, not dogma demons stuffing facts down their throats. It follows that the trauma of exams will be a thing of the past. We shall once and for all lead the Nation into a trouble-free world of free-thinkers. Yes! That's the way! At One Together, my friends!'

Once again the audience smothered their leader in praise. How could they fail with such embracing care? Stalin slapped his knees, his laughter echoed around the auditorium. Tancredi tried to quieten him; he knew they would soon be in trouble.

'This next measure,' the Leader continued, looking serene, 'will disappoint those who are fond of their own aggrandisement.'

There was distaste and ridicule in his voice. He fixed Stalin with a stare. He had been considering the policy he was about to announce for some time. When he had first recognised the interloper in the front row, he had controlled his shock masterfully. Now that his speech had become a battle of wills with the Russian dictator, he drew on his powers of improvisation to deliver a body-blow.

'Today I announce a revolution in the naming of public places.'

Stalin refolded his arms, and listened attentively. There was a hint of a smile around his mouth as he prepared for further amusement. The Leader assumed a po-face.

'Too many places are offensively named after so-called great men, military victories or some point of local ethnicity. Our new system will be based on grid references, for example, "I live at 001567." It's the logical conclusion of the postcode system. Place names will also perform a useful social function. They will no longer be the decadent celebration of a single person or act, but will instead have meaning for the whole of society.'

He leant over the lectern, challenging any contradiction to his logic.

'People will rejoice to be living in Disabled Street or Income Support Row.'

Stalin merely gawped, unable to respond. This latest statement of policy was beyond his comprehension.

'I'd like to finish with a story, something I heard a few days ago, one that beggars belief in this day and age.'

The Leader paused so his audience could change gear from presentation to parable.

'The following is true. I haven't embellished a single word for dramatic effect. I have no desire to wow you. Just the honest, simple and sad truth.'

He leant over the lectern to gather in his flock, and stared into the middle distance, his face a picture of plaintive misery. This was going to be a difficult piece.

'The story begins with the Zamosky family, two working parents with two children. Margarita is a care worker in a learning support centre, Frederick is the mother of the family looking after the kids at home. A happy family with everything to live for.'

'Frederick and Margarita take their six-year-old Felix to the superstore for the weekly shop, leaving his brother at home watching an educational programme on television. The family wanders the aisles with a long list of items.'

'Felix gets bored and asks if he can go and play conkers with the other children beside a horse chestnut tree outside the store. He is mature for his age, top of his class. His parents trust him, they give permission. They are a forward-thinking family, keen to extend a sense of carefree responsibility to their off-spring.'

'Felix is active, full of energy and life. He finds a monster conker and borrows a skewer and string from a teenage boy. Soon he's wielding his weapon against an opponent in a vicious conker competition.'

'He smashes successive conkers and reaches the final. It's against the teenager who gave him the string. Both bash away, their conkers refuse to smash. But the teenager is stronger and delivers a forceful blow. Felix's conker fires backwards out of control and strikes him on the forehead. Instantly he drops to the ground.'

The audience shuddered at the thought, a wave of shared pain and sympathy flowed through the hall. The Leader's voice sounded constricted when he continued. His hands came up to cover his moist eyes, then slid down to his mouth in a symbol of prayer. He paused, coughed to clear his emotions, and looked up again at the sea of faces to share their anguish.

'Felix Zamosky died in hospital two days later. He never regained consciousness. He wasn't able to say goodbye to his parents. They couldn't say goodbye to him.'

His voice began to crack.

'Now answer me this.'

His moistened eyes swept the hall; his figure seemed to swell on the podium.

'There are no safety regulations to govern children playing conkers. Why?'

He again roamed the faces before him seeking an answer.

'Because we lack the zeal to regulate conker competitions. Yet clearly this is what's needed – full protective clothing, conkers assessed for size and strength in relation to the ages of children competing. All to be supervised by an adult monitor trained in physics, with passports produced by children to match them against same age competitors, written permission from parents, paramedics at hand.'

'The Law to encompass exclusion for any gathering of less than fifty children to ensure proper organisation. All competitions to be booked with local authorities three months in advance with suitable risk assessment and venue allocation determinants. Special regulations to ensure the disabled receive proper consideration.'

He raised his voice, a priest about to harangue his congregation.

'After we're re-elected, I will conduct a root-and-branch review of health and safety.'

He paused; the audience sensed he was on the brink of making a pledge.

'There is a whole raft of legislative issues here. We will commit the resources, regardless of cost, to protecting all our citizens, all of the time. We will remove all obstacles to intensive direct social care by the State. This I promise. This is our commitment to the Nation! At One Together!'

The Russian dictator doubled up. Tears of laughter streamed down his face. Tancredi stood up and took hold of his arm. He had to get him out, but it was too late. The Leader nodded and a band of men wearing protective gloves, goggles and orange boiler suits were upon them. As one took hold of the lapels of Stalin's coat, he sprang from his seat with surprising agility. Seconds later there was an ear-splitting crunch as Stalin brought his head into his assailant's face, pulping his nose.

The front of the auditorium descended into a mêlée of flying fists, in
which Tancredi found himself swinging with his missing
arm. The Russian bear and his disabled companion
were soon overpowered.

'Bring them,' said the Leader,
sweeping off the
podium.

XX

THE NEW

MIDDLE WAY

Now we're in trouble,' said Tancredi as they were bundled down a corridor.

'Nonsense,' Stalin replied, 'the man's a weakling, without morals, as changeable as the wind. The "Middle Way" isn't policy, it's a marketing ploy. He'll bend to my will in minutes.'

'I fear your travels in time and space have affected your mind,' said Tancredi. 'This isn't Russia before the revolution. Correctomondo is an advanced society, whatever your opinion of its politics. There's a difference between short-termism and lack of principle.'

'You're naïve,' came the curt reply. 'They're one and the same. And political correctness comes in many flavours. The Leader has a taste for the most pungent – personal failure suffused with jealousy. There are no depths of idiocy to which he will not descend – who will dare argue? Surely you can see that this system is spiralling into ever more self-defeating circles?'

Presently a door was flung open and they were marched into a palatial room with a magnificent view of Pious, the capital of Correctomondo. Crystal chandeliers hung from the ceiling, gold leaf adorned the walls, and the floor was of the finest marble. Assistants, all eager young political types, stood in clusters around the chamber. Tancredi thought the surroundings opulent given the modesty of the Leader. Stalin snorted and rolled his eyes. As they entered the room they caught sight of the Leader, his back turned to them, looking out of the window.

'I know who you are,' he said without bothering to turn towards them. 'A man of evil, a monster, a ...'

'To some,' Stalin cut in, not allowing him to finish his pre-planned diatribe. 'A hero to others.'

He glanced at Tancredi, who glimpsed a hint of humour in his eyes.

'Do you think that men wake up calculating how to do evil? Isn't one man's crime another man's ideal? Or is it easier to believe that there are square answers, one formula that will make the world a better place?'

The Leader wasn't accustomed to philosophical debate: his skill was in the art of the correct. He decided to retreat to safer ground. His entourage pretended to be busy; in fact they were tuned into the unusual situation developing.

'So you ridicule the politics of the Middle Way? The language of centrality, fairness and consideration spoken in Correctomondo.'

139

He turned towards his adversary, unable to sustain his window-gazing pose.

'But not understood elsewhere,' Stalin replied in overt disgust.

He moved a few steps towards him, unfastening the top button of his coat.

'Did the Romans, rulers of the world, operate according to your criteria? And were the Spartans a middle-of-the-road sort of people? By definition you repudiate anything great.'

The Leader sneered as he sized up the square-shouldered Russian in his old-fashioned coat. He had him now, he could recite the creed which had defined his life and propelled him to power.

'Greatness no longer exists. It has been abolished alongside ideology. Everything has coalesced into the middle. Caesar is no longer a general – he's a manager.'

Tancredi was surprised by the cogency of his response. There were less great issues, and those which existed were dealt with in collaboration by interplanetary bodies. The Universe was ruled by consensus. Stalin huffed, his face betraying the irritation of an adult reasoning with an obdurate child.

'Pah! Fool! Don't you tire of standing in the centre? Of watching every word for fear of a slip? Of weighing each situation by what is expedient rather than by what you believe? Of not taking risks? Of being a slave to the sound bite?'

The Leader opened his mouth to reply; Stalin continued, raising his hand to silence him.

'And let's say power is achieved based on a platform of the Middle Way. What's the point? You can't act beyond tinkering at the edges. You're unable to grasp the painful issues which need to be grasped. They are allowed to fester. Is your aim merely to achieve the median position, so that in old age you can remind yourself, and those few people still interested in you, that once you were yet another irrelevant leader?'

The Leader laughed, but Tancredi detected some nervousness. Since they were now engaged in a discussion about realpolitik, the Leader decided to lower his guard. The pretence of honesty could be disarming.

'And how do you propose I would be elected in the first place? Do you believe people will tick a box marked "pain"? The purpose of politics is power. We live in a comfortable age where extremes no longer exist. You do whatever it takes, sometimes holding opposite views simultaneously. You know that.'

Tancredi understood the necessity of pragmatism in public life. On the other hand, what was the point of politics if not to be bold and drive change? And what was the balance between pragmatism, which risked stasis, and idealism, which could lead to oblivion? Stalin, the street fighter, decided to turn things up a notch.

'So you intend to inspire the crowd with high-flown, pre-tested words like "fairness", "change" and "values". A clear sign that you've nothing of interest to say beyond the sterilised speech, the words of a goody-goody, beneath contempt.'

Stalin removed his cap and ruffled his thick hair.

'Words must be measured, opinions balanced, to draw the people in,' the Leader replied. 'I emote with my children at the breakfast table in front of television cameras. The electorate see a mug with the words "Best Dad"; they believe. I spend hours being coached on what to say and how to look.'

'Pathetic!' shouted the dictator, strutting towards him. 'You fear anything untried, terrified that something you say might boomerang back against you, that someone somewhere might object. That you won't be able to provide an answer which is sufficiently bland if challenged. That to show leadership in thought – or anything but putrid nothingness – will undermine your power base. You're not a leader, you're a lap-dog. Your existence defines a new quality of human emptiness. You're a mere shadow of a mouse!'

The Leader's attendants shuffled uneasily. Some heads nodded as Stalin spoke. They had never before seen the imperturbable Leader under fire, and he wasn't winning the argument.

'People are lazy,' the Leader shrieked, upset and red-faced. 'They don't want to make decisions. They only absorb so much, simple ideas that create a reaction, not a thought. Politics is spectacle, not substance. You do whatever it takes.'

143

He glared at his opponent. He had climbed the ladder without a slip, he knew how things worked. Maybe there had once been a role for greatness in public life, but not any more. Politics was a profession. Politicians had no other 'job'. You did your time, after which you wrote a biography filled with obvious insights and remorse for opportunities missed. Then you filled your boots with appropriate sinecures. This was the way of things.

Yet deep down he knew there was a flaw in his thinking. Although a fanatic, he was able to recognise when he took positions to be heard or adopted policies for effect. In doing so he was storing up a deficit of integrity which could only be concealed in the perpetual scramble to sustain himself. But the pretence was tiring. The Russian's expert assault was now drawing the sensation he most dreaded to the surface of his consciousness – fear of exposure.

'Of course,' Stalin shot back with growing sarcasm, 'short-term success is preferable by far to long-term conviction. Pathetic intellectual coward! Politically correct prude! Pampered poodle to mediocrity! You think you'll be remembered for feeble moralising blandishments? You deprived piece of historic ash. There's no longer a flame! You have burnt! Has it ever occurred to you that real leadership involves the defiance of conventional wisdom, breaking the rules?'

Tancredi was surprised to find himself agreeing with Stalin. There seemed to be no point to the Leader. He imagined a universe where a drug was administered to all those in positions of power, inducing continuous bold behaviour. The Leader of Correctomondo had achieved his position, but so what? Although Stalin was like a siege gun, relentlessly pounding its target, his basic philosophy – moving forward, speaking out, taking risks – chimed with Tancredi's view of life.

'What about another approach,' he cut in, trying to balance the Russian's blitzkrieg with a positive suggestion, 'a New Middle Way?'

To Tancredi's surprise, the bombast agreed.

'Exactly,' rejoined Stalin, deftly picking up the idea, 'what else is the Middle Way if not all things to all people? It is whatever you want it to be to suit the situation. The New Middle Way. Exploit your position.'

This wasn't exactly what Tancredi had meant, but they needed to shift the Leader's focus to a longer-term horizon. The Leader fell silent, hurt and brooding. He brought his hand to his chin, thinking about re-casting his political creed. He knew he had been overwhelmed.

But what if the fearsome Russian was right? There was nothing wrong with adjusting his position; change was one of his favourite words. It made sense. What worked one day could be discarded the next in the name of progress. His attendants moved closer, anticipating that they might be needed to support him in some great act.

'But how can this be achieved?' he asked sulkily.

He was still trying to resist his tormentor, but there was a breech.

'You were elected on a platform of the Middle Way,' Stalin continued, 'now you must sustain your power in the face of a serious challenge. The Middle Way was consensual. The New Middle Way is vigorous.'

With this, the dictator slammed his bunched fist into the palm of his other hand.

'Previously you used words and compromised. Now you wield a bludgeon and insist. Times have changed – re-make your politics. What could be more natural? Breathe new life into the tired beast.'

'I'm not sure that's entirely ...' began Tancredi.

'Nonsense!' interrupted Stalin.

He strode towards the Leader and grasped him by the shoulders.

'There's a mighty burden upon your shoulders.' His eyes bored into the Leader. 'You may be ridiculed, even vilified. So be it. History is made by doers, people who are prepared to sacrifice themselves for the greater good. Society needs history to progress. You must lead your people through the heart of darkness, and bring them to a better place. Fill the vacuum of nihility with a new purpose. Carpe diem! Courage, little kitten! Let's hear your lion's roar!'

Now Tancredi was uneasy. In joining in the debate, he had intended to preach the merits of long-term thinking, not Bolshevik revolt. The Leader appeared to be collapsing in the face of Stalin's attack. As he asked 'What must I do?', Tancredi no longer seemed to be part of the conversation.

Stalin held the Leader close, his breath besmirching the rose-scented skin of his face.

'Using your security forces,' he said, emphasising each word. 'You must eliminate all those who stand against you. You will do this with the best possible intentions, in a caring sort of way.'

'No!' screamed Tancredi.

'Onwards!' shouted Stalin, punching his fist in the air.

'Ruthlessness without fear of retribution! Forward with me! Forward to the New Middle Way! '

All eyes were on the Leader; there was total silence. Agonising seconds passed. He had lived his whole life in modest self-denial, knowing always that this moment would come. The call to greatness. The Russian was no longer his interlocutor, but his liberator. Now he too would be remembered, with streets and city squares named in his honour.

The Leader nodded his head. The room erupted. His entourage tore about the chamber, screeching orders, summoning officials. Tancredi's further scream of 'Nooo!' was drowned out by loud Russian laughter rising above the commotion.

'So much for the Middle Way, my innocent friend,' Stalin shouted.

He strode over and clapped Tancredi on the shoulder. Then Tancredi was swept out of the room as the party of the New Middle Way prepared to fulfil its new-found ambition.

After a fast-paced sleigh ride he was back at the Professor's hideout in the cold wilderness. A space rocket stood outside. Cocomo and Kasbek raced up to him. Tamany was busy wrapping the bedpan, fool's hat and methane pannier into Tancredi's game show cloak; he secured the package with his pin from the *Invincible*.

'Quick, we're leaving immediately,' Tancredi panted, taking Cocomo by the hand.

The Professor looked startled.

'I regret to inform you that your planet is about to enter a new phase in its history,' Tancredi said, propelling his group towards the rocket. 'Political correctness is about to be redefined.'

Everyone clambered on board. As the Professor tried to remonstrate with Tancredi, he spotted a Star of Lenin stuck to his shoulder.

'What's that?' he asked.

Tancredi looked down and noticed it for the first time.

'For idiocy,' he replied.

Tamany waved Kasbek's paw at the confused-looking
Professor as Tancredi lifted the
rocket into space.

XXI
COMFORTABLY
NUMB

For the first time the travellers could choose their next destination. Tancredi thought he might at last avoid being humiliated, exploited or eaten. Space was full of rumours about the impending explosion of Surprise. On Correctomondo, Tancredi had seen instructions, together with a diagram, on correct form for a can-can: back straight, hands on hips, kicks to waist height. All across the Universe people were practising the dance.

With the end of humanity in sight, Cocomo agreed a deal with Tamany. Since childhood she had wanted to experience a party on the planet Comfortably Numb. Now seemed her best and only chance. She would teach Tamany to pilot the rocket; in return he would deposit them on the planet.

On approaching Comfortably Numb, the landing site was obvious to the new pilot. It was early evening; beneath them was a crowd waiting to enter an amphitheatre of Roman design with magnificent columns and vaulted arches. Its carved coral stonework was covered in ivy; torches attached to its exterior gave off a shimmering light.

Tamany set the craft to hover inches above the crowd's head, and Cocomo and Tancredi disembarked onto a sea of raised hands. As he was deposited on the ground Tancredi breathed a sigh of relief for the first time since leaving Earth. He was in an atmosphere of relaxed euphoria, about to spend a night with the woman he loved.

Comfortably Numb occupied a unique position in the Universe. The planet consisted of a solitary tropical island surrounded by an azure sea. Party-goers from all over the Cosmos flocked to its white beaches. During the day, they would lie in the sunshine. At sunset, they congregated at beach bars to watch the kaleidoscopic light show, following which the entertainment began.

The gravitational force of the amphitheatre had a strange effect on those outside. Tancredi noticed that people sped up as they approached; the psychology on arrival was to hurry. He and Cocomo were caught in a wave of party-goers pushing through its entrance tunnel. This featured a holographic display of a flock of white swans being chased by a black swan to the accompaniment of a cascading orchestral score. Arriving inside the arena, Cocomo clapped her hands with excitement. Tancredi hadn't imagined that such a show of pleasure from the cool-headed warrioress was possible.

The amphitheatre was lit by thousands of motorised light bulbs, all the size and shape of cygnets. These were programmed to swoop and swirl in the air above the heads of the audience, flapping their wings in a perpetual ballet. They were beautiful to watch. Cocomo looked upwards, open-mouthed.

Tancredi put his arm around her. He felt sublime. Not only was she the most exquisite girl in the Universe, she'd also shown him how to give life to his creed. And now he saw a new side to her. He knew he was weak in matters of the heart, quick to confer the status of soulmate on a new fancy, but if Cocomo wasn't the girl of his dreams, then who could be?

As they mingled with the crowd, Tancredi became aware of people glancing and pointing at him. News of his adventures had spread. In a universe dedicated to short-termism, his altruistic mission was confusing; he had become notorious. People were interested in him, particularly in the more gruesome details of his exploits. The party-goers now examined this rough-looking man, unshaven with tangled hair, a missing limb, and a beauty queen on his arm. Tancredi swelled with pride.

Cocomo's feelings for Tancredi were more circumspect. The journey from disdain to passion was too great for her to make in a single leap. She needed to pause for breath on the verge of strong attachment. The party atmosphere quickened her pace of travel. Still, she maintained the reserve which was her hallmark.

It was a warm summer's night. Tancredi guided Cocomo through the throng to the centre of the amphitheatre. Momentarily the cygnets extinguished their lights, plunging the party-goers into darkness. 'Watch out!' a loud speaker announced as a holographic black swan swept fast and low over the crowd. Its detailing was spectacular, each feather a work of art. The creature's wings stretched the width of the arena, the golden flash of its breath swept overhead.

The crowd gasped, then screamed as the swan plucked a girl from the audience and carried her off into the night sky.

Seconds later it re-appeared and found another victim. Soon dozens of girls were being snatched and spirited away. The crowd scattered in every direction. Girls screamed as each victim was snatched. The boys held the girls close, trying to anticipate the next abduction. The heroic gestures amused Tancredi. Resistance to the black swan was futile, the more so because its prey were holographic projections like itself.

The swan ceased its attack; the airborne cygnets brightened, signalling the party was about to begin. A single electronic note rang out, hard and malignant, a portent of danger ahead. The crowd reacted with wolf whistles and shouts, then looked up to see a DJ sporting the head, neck and wings of a black swan, flying as if by magic through the air. His keyboard swung like a guitar from his shoulder.

The note sounded again. The cygnets swarmed around the DJ, only to be beaten back by another note. They retreated to the top of the stadium where they turned their lights upwards. A great sail spread overhead, extinguishing the night sky. As the crowd roared, the sound reflected back, then bounced around the arena.

The electronic note was followed by another, then another. The crowd started to cheer. Eventually the note morphed into a simple bass-line, continuously repeated. The crowd clapped, the cygnet lights flashed in time to the music.

Cocomo beamed and beat time with the surrounding throng. The visceral thump of the bass-line continued to loop, pulsating in her gut. Everyone was waiting for it to change. The second it did, the arena would explode. The crowd began to jump in time to the beat. Magically, the bass-line had transformed a crowd of thousands into a single entity.

And then it happened: the bass-line changed. The crowd gave a unified visceral roar, creating a ripple in the overhead sail. The sound ricocheted back down to the ground. The amphitheatre became a cauldron of leaping bodies, Cocomo the most energetic. A group of admirers formed around her. She was the most beautiful woman ever to have visited the planet. As Cocomo moved to the music, a smartly dressed man, athletic and well built, danced up to her. He smiled radiantly, introduced himself above the noise of Soloman. He handed her an invitation which read: 'After party – Ylang Ylang'.

The DJ circled overhead. There was still no melody or verse, just a hard beat that gripped the crowd in its hypnotic thrall. The cygnets were banished skywards and a murky gloom settled over the arena. Now the DJ summoned a flock of black swans, who took the form of female dancers swarming about him in the air. It was impossible to discern what kept them aloft. The bodies of Brazilian beach dancers, oiled and stunning, were revealed beneath swan's wings, heads and necks. In an instant, thousands of men below activated infrared glasses, and the audience lit up like luminous algae.

The swan dance was athletic, a combination of rapid hip shakes and sensual sliding steps. The rhythm increased in tempo, the girls somersaulted in the air, then recovered to the hip-shaking position. A jungle drum took up the beat, adding a tribal intensity to the dance. Tancredi and Cocomo were no more than microbes in a sea of flesh, gyrating to the command of the DJ and his dancers. They moved together, bodies touching, waiting for some relief from the beat.

The dancers formed a circle around the DJ. He stretched out his arms, bestowing the benediction of the black swan. They raised their wings towards him, hips shaking in a gesture of veneration. The drumbeat intensified, maracas and castanets joining in the rhythm. The girls turned in circles, pushed their groins forward in simulated copulation. This was the climax, the crowd moaned their lust. The dancers suffered agonies, their movements became violent, grotesque. The crowd responded, jumping as a great singularity, maniacal, demented. A scream rose above the bass-line as a veil of blackness spread across the arena.

Suddenly a shaft of light permeated the gloom. The cygnets had returned from exile. They buzzed about, attacking the black swan DJ and his dancing cohort. Out of nowhere a giant white swan descended, and the cygnets went supernova in a burst of blindingly brilliant whiteness. At last the bass-line climaxed, a great swell of synthesised strings, music of light and hope echoed through the amphitheatre.

As the forces of good broke through the darkness, a white mist emitted from the white swan's beak. It swirled in the air above the party-goers. As if on command, it dropped like rain and dissipated amongst the crowd.

Tancredi and Cocomo felt an incredible lightness. Their bodies started to tingle. Laughter rang out as the crowd began to move with grace. Some traced ballet steps on the dance floor. Others performed a can-can in slow motion, with exaggerated sinuous gestures. There was more laughter in mockery of the antidote to Armageddon.

The euphoric feeling infected minds as well as bodies. Tancredi was already in love with Cocomo, but the white mist gave his emotions an indescribable urgency. His love transformed into the incredible. As the strings rose in volume, the party-goers again began to dance; this time in couples, not as a crowd. Tancredi buried his head in Cocomo's black hair and closed his eyes.

When he opened them he noticed a nearby couple climbing aboard a white swan parked on the floor of the amphitheatre. It was the size of a small bed, with a padded back, strewn with cushions. He watched in amazement as it flapped its wings and began to ascend skywards. Soon there were dozens of white swans floating above the crowd.

Tancredi took Cocomo's hand and led her off to a swan. The ascent upwards was spectacular but also, for some reason, hysterical. They looked down. The amphitheatre was a mosaic of dancing bodies, flying swans and cygnets darting in every direction. It was the most beautiful sight he'd ever seen, the best moment of his life.

In a heartbeat, he disavowed his beliefs. Introspection, self-awareness, thoughtfulness be damned. How misguided he had been. It was all absurd. He would willingly embrace the cult of short-termism, epitomised by the narcotic, if only it would last forever.

The swan closed its wings and they were encased in a white paradise. It

was programmed to stop when it reached the top of the

amphitheatre. Inexplicably it failed to do so.

The swan described circles in the

air as it climbed into

space.

XXII
YLANG
YLANG

O f all the swans floating above Comfortably Numb that night, Tamany guessed that the one which had strayed into space must contain his friends. Immediately, he launched a rescue mission, and the travellers were soon reunited on the rocket. They gathered around its console, which told them Surprise would go supernova within hours. They decided to await the end of the Universe on terra firma.

Still euphoric from the all-night festivities, Cocomo remembered her invitation to Ylang Ylang. Where better to spend their last hours than in the calming atmosphere of an after-party? Tamany set a course for the nearby planet. As they touched down on the new world, they knew that this would be their final destination.

Once the drug had worn off, Tancredi again felt mixed emotions. On the one hand he was in love; he felt a happiness he'd never imagined. His travels had been worthwhile for this alone. On the other, he had failed in his mission, which was now at an end. He had also been party to genocide, a shocking thought. The wounds he sustained on Sanitalis and Obesitas were nothing compared to the catastrophe which had befallen Correctomondo. Although dejected by failure, he comforted himself with the thought that he would die with the girl he loved.

The rocket provided scant information on the planet, which was a world of jungles and deserts, populated by different tribes. Tancredi and his companions found themselves in a garden of cacti with pretty pink and purple blooms. A stream of crystal water flowed through its centre, prehistoric stones decorated the landscape.

They set off into the garden in search of Soloman and soon came to a children's play area featuring a battered tea-cup ride. Beyond was the mouth of a cave with a boulder, which served as its door, rolled to one side. A window with iron bars was set into the rock face, giving a view of its interior. A group of impoverished children wearing the yellow and brown shuka of desert tribespeople were kicking around. They were supervised by some sad-looking women, presumably their mothers. Oblivious to the poverty of the scene, Tamany and Kasbek raced over to join them.

Only one of the children would play with Tamany, a pretty girl with sparkling brown eyes set in a dark-skinned face who introduced herself as Solange. Tancredi chuckled – everywhere he travelled, there was always one to stand out from the crowd. Differentiation should be taught at school; it was superior by far to science, maths or history.

Shortly Soloman came bounding through the garden towards them. He was still in his party clothes of leopard-skin trousers and an expensive silk shirt.

He waved a muscular arm in the air by way of greeting.

'I'm so happy you came,' he boomed. 'Welcome to Ylang Ylang! Welcome to our paradise! Welcome to the after party!'

His face lit up as he saw Cocomo, and he smiled a smile of dazzling whiteness.

'This is the General's garden. These are his people. The party's at his palace. Please, come with me.'

By now Tamany was engaged in a staring competition with Solange. The game had occupied him and Kasbek for hours during their travels, gazing into each other's eyes to see who would blink first. Tamany always won, following which Kasbek would fall into a deep sleep. Tancredi couldn't disturb the combat now it had begun, so he promised to return soon.

Tancredi and Cocomo followed Soloman along a garden path. Tancredi felt strangely bold. Love had made him confident, but he also knew he needed to show courage in the face of what was about to happen. Cocomo wasn't afraid of the coming Armageddon. As he walked in the sunshine he felt her equal. He would play his part when the time came.

Soloman strode along humming a merry tune, emitting an occasional chuckle. The extraordinary beauty of the planet seemed to Tancredi to be at odds with the poverty of the people they passed. He interrupted his host's reverie to enquire about this surprising contradiction.

'You have a sharp eye,' Soloman roared, slapping him on the back as if they were old friends, 'but if we weren't destitute, we wouldn't get funding.'

He threw back his head and laughed a deep-throated laugh. Tancredi continued to look bemused.

'You're aware that every planet exists for a purpose?' Soloman continued his explanation with a patronising smile. 'Sanitalis is for health, Comfortably Numb for the relaxation of no tomorrows, Eros One for a reason I need not describe.'

Tancredi nodded, he understood this much.

'Ylang Ylang is the custodian of the Galaxy's guilt. We embrace it, my friend. Politicians and pop stars come here to emote against backdrops of bloated bellies and beautiful staring eyes. Naturally, we charge a fortune for this service.'

'But what's the benefit to them?'

'All those in positions of power and influence,' Soloman exclaimed, throwing his arms in the air, 'must burnish their caring credentials with a visit to the planet. It's a basic requirement. They moan with the destitute. They weep with our wanting. They are horrified by the helpless hunger.'

This appeared to Tancrdi to be the epitome of thoughtlessness.

'But if the planet is paid to remain in this sad condition,' he said quizzically, 'how will its people progress?'

Soloman sighed as if trapped into giving a lesson in the rudimentary facts of life. Then he beamed another glittering smile. The General's palace was some way distant; he would indulge his guest.

'Who refuses cash? To be looked after? Enwrapped by the care and compassion of donor planets, why should we fritter away time and effort doing things for ourselves?'

Presently they came to a clearing in the garden which gave a view over a great hole in the ground. It appeared to be a mine of some sort. Hundreds of workers wearing ragged clothes were busy toiling in the sunshine. Cocomo stopped to look.

'I see Ylang Ylang has wealth,' she said.

'Indeed,' Soloman replied, 'but the mine doesn't belong to us.'

'Foreign powers again?' asked Cocomo. 'That sounds like exploitation.'

'Years ago you would have been right, pretty lady,' Soloman replied, delighted to be talking to Cocomo. 'Now you're wrong.'

'In ages past Ylang Ylang was brutalised by neighbouring worlds. They stole our resources, subverted our culture, enslaved our populace. Then times changed and civilisation progressed. The situation today is completely different.'

'Ylang Ylang remains rich in resources, which it's only natural for other planets to covet. But today, instead of enslaving us, they talk wonderfully about active engagement, positive partnerships, benefits for all. Then they take the mines.'

'There are many types of exploitation,' Cocomo replied. 'This looks like the ethical kind.'

Soloman howled with laughter.

They carried on down the path and came to an area covered in tarmac on which was parked a dizzying array of military machines and exotic luxury cars — jeeps, tanks, trucks, helicopters, and fighter planes were reflected in the waxed gloss of Lamborghinis, Boxters and Silver Shadows. A private jet glistened in the sunlight. Tancredi and Cocomo were amazed by the display. Soloman stood by proudly.

'Behold the power of Ylang Ylang,' he said, ignoring the ephemeral luxury.

'How can you afford such things?' Tancredi asked. 'Shouldn't the funds be spent on alleviating the poverty of your people?'

Soloman spread out his arms to embrace the hardware before them.

'Without security,' he smiled benignly at his student of the Universe, 'there would be no poverty to protect. But there's another benefit. Acquiring weapons provides another opportunity to work with our benefactors from other worlds. As a practical planet, we also test them as often as possible.'

'As for the jet, our leader aspires to a better life for all. He leads by example. All you see before you is a sign of progress. Now we all want a better life.'

Shortly, the path opened onto a lawn at the end of which stood a palace built of brick, which shone like gold in the sunlight.

'This is the General's house,' said Soloman as they walked up the lawn.

The palace doors were guarded by menacing-looking soldiers. Their dress was slovenly, but they sported all manner of aggressive weaponry. The group was admitted into an inner courtyard with a fountain playing in the middle. Tancredi was amazed such a building existed in so desolate a place. Despite its grandeur, it was strewn with debris. Soloman took them down a corridor lined with palm trees in broken pots. A pair of carved doors, pockmarked with graffiti, swung open; a blast of disco music greeted them.

The General was sitting with one leg slung over the arm of a gold throne, which resembled a pantomime prop. He wore a pair of military camouflage trousers, no shoes or shirt, and a red bandana across his forehead. A deep scar ran from his abdomen to his lower lip, as if he'd been cleaved like a piece of cheese. His left eye was murky white. He was surrounded by milky vapours which looked like clouds of stage smoke. Then the smell hit Tancredi. It was the effluence of a dozen drug bongs being smoked by a group of children surrounding the throne. They touted automatic rifles as large as their skeletal bodies, with ammunition belts hung over their skinny torsos for clothing.

A great cheer went up as Soloman paraded his guests into the throne room. Tancredi stepped in front of Cocomo in a protective reflex; he looked at Soloman stupefied.

'What else did you expect?'
Soloman beamed.

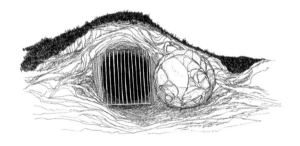

XXIII
THE
ABYSS

In a heartbeat the child soldiers surrounded them.

'So Soloman man, what you bring me?' asked the General.

Soloman smiled his dazzling smile.

The answer was obvious, as Cocomo emerged from behind her protector. The General's eyes bulged.

'A real beauty,' were the last words Tancredi heard.

Suddenly he was on the ground; he'd been struck in the stomach. He looked up, gasping for breath. The General and Cocomo had vanished.

A pain shot up his leg, his ankle crushed by a rifle butt. He kicked violently with his free leg, and was hit again. A boy placed a boot on his face. He began to suffocate, and terrible rasping came from the back of his throat. Another child joined in the attack, strafing him with an ammunition belt. The pain was excruciating. Lacerations opened all over his body. The soldiers began to dance around their victim shrieking a drug-crazed cry. Tancredi curled into a ball, trying to protect himself with his good arm. He was hit again, and blacked out.

Night had fallen when Tancredi was awakened by a jolt. The ground was shaking beneath him. Moonlight streamed through the throne-room windows, illuminating the scene of his torment. He was in agony; he had no idea how many bones had been broken. Instantly he thought of Cocomo. His face flushed hot, he was about to panic; he had to find her. He forced himself up and lurched out of the throne room, dragging his foot behind him. When he reached the courtyard, he was again thrown to the ground. Surprise was about to go supernova. The Universe was beginning to implode.

He staggered out of the palace. The guards had abandoned their posts and linked arms, about to perform the death-defying dance. Tancredi laughed through his pain. He hauled himself down the lawn and found the pathway. There he stumbled across a body. Knowing immediately who it was, he fell to his knees.

Tancredi took Cocomo in his arms, wiping the blood-stained hair from her face. He hung his head low, breathing in her smell, and buried his face in the torn clothes on her chest. He gasped. He couldn't breathe, an unbearable pressure was building within. Tears streamed down his face. His body tensed, then came the release. A burst of agony issued into the night sky, the sound of a breaking heart in a broken body, Tancredi calling to Cocomo.

The planet began to convulse. He couldn't stand to think about what had happened, then he remembered Tamany. He looked at Cocomo's beautiful face illuminated by the moonlight. He would carry this image with him in the few minutes remaining. He kissed her for the last time.

Tancredi forced himself up, and limped down the path. His mind was blank, numb with pain. The best he could do was listen out for sounds like a primitive beast. He picked up distant screams, and followed them to the play area where he had left his friends. He stumbled towards a group of women gathered at the cave, enclosed now by the boulder. They were clinging onto one another, pounding on the rock, shrieking in hysterics.

'What's happened?' shouted Tancredi. 'Are the children trapped?'

The women pointed to the window. Tancredi rushed over to look. The cave's interior was dimly lit, but he could see the children within. They were running about screaming. He caught sight of Tamany, clearly panic-stricken. He yelled at him, rapping on the window. Then he saw the cause of the children's consternation. The General was in the cave, stumbling around as if drunk, grabbing at the children.

Tancredi struck again at the window, this time in rage. The General looked up and their eyes met. He laughed, then lunged at Solange and caught hold of her yellow and brown shuka. As a shockwave rocked the planet, the General locked his arm around her neck. Solange screamed and writhed in his grasp. Tancredi felt sick. With all his heart he wanted to tear at the beast.

The planet's vibrations worsened. Cracks appeared in the rock. The women realised a child had been caught. A cry went up and they fell to the ground, beating it with their hands. Tancredi looked back through the window. Bile rose in his mouth. The General was holding Solange by her hair. He knelt before her, bent back her neck, then opened his mouth.

Finally, on the brink of extinction, this was it. The abyss. A continuum of thoughtlessness. The coalescing of everything most foul in a dark cave on a rotten planet where thinking didn't exist. So why should evil have an end?

Tancredi staggered backwards, unable to watch. This was beyond words, beyond comprehension, beyond madness. He stumbled about mindlessly, as if drugged, his sense of defeat complete. The twilight of the world had reduced visibility to a murky fog. He fell head-first into a spinning tea cup which contained the package of his possessions kept by Tamany. The ground trembled against the Satanic forces of destruction. Great fissures opened in the earth. Cocomo was dead, Tamany trapped, Kasbek lost, Solange – he couldn't bear to think – and he was coiled, pathetic, in a spinning tea cup.

Tancredi took a final decision. He attached the methane pannier to the back of the teacup. As Ylang Ylang began to disintegrate, he ignited the gas and shot off the planet towards Surprise.

XXIV
SURPRISE

All across the Universe people linked arms. On Sanitalis, the monster stopped his ravages and joined arms with an invalid. The populace of Eros Two came together in the divorce stadium. The man-pigs of Scoop oinked into a kicking formation. On Obesitas, the bulky inhabitants hovered about the Game Show Hall, stretching out fleshy limbs. The people of Correctomondo donned safety gloves and formed a line. On Comfortably Numb, the party-goers joined in for fun. The tribes of Ylang Ylang congregated in circles in the desert, they would kick the highest. On Earth, across green fields and grey cities, people linked arms.

Surprise was ringed by satellites for the occasion. Billions of eyes were focussed on the moment of explosion, the signal to begin the can-can. These same eyes now saw a lone figure in a spinning teacup, hurtling towards the star. Next, they witnessed the figure collapse. Something had come alive and toppled Tancredi. Kasbek shook himself from sleep and stood up to face the end of the Universe with his master.

A strange energy came off the star as they approached, infusing Tancredi's possessions with an unexpected result. Tamany's pin transformed into a sword, the Matron's bedpan became a shield, the fool's cap from Eros turned into a helmet. As Tancredi tore towards Surprise, Obesitan game show cloak streaming in his wake, he was bathed in a red glow that emanated from the Star of Lenin given to him on Correctomondo.

Tancredi and Kasbek landed on Surprise, a sea of fires and lava flows. The ground shook with the power of ten thousand earthquakes, and fierce winds swept the face of the star. Tancredi, protected by his martial outfit, looked down at Kasbek sheltered beneath his shield and stroked his head for the last time. This is what he had always wanted: to face death standing, weapon in hand. The Universe watched as he raised his sword and strode into the heart of the inferno. He was last seen bending into the wind, Kasbek by his side, a great fireball of light thundering towards him.

Surprise went supernova. There was a second of calm, then an ear-splitting blast which echoed across time and space. Gigantic concentric circles of energy radiated out from the star as billions of legs performed a can-can. The wave engulfed everything in its path, knocked over the dancers mid-kick, after which everything went dark. The boom of the supernova dissipated. The Universe fell silent for the first time since Creation.

Then, out of the darkness, billions of points of light descended. They spread like rainfall across the Universe touching everybody on every planet. Simultaneously, all humanity experienced exactly the same realisation.

Everyone knew with perfect certainty that they were going to die. The thought became as fundamental as breathing. With this, the utter futility of so much human behaviour became clear. What was the point of chasing money, power, prestige, unless for a higher purpose? Nothing survives the grave. What reason was there to hold extreme views which lead nowhere? History only celebrates the humane. Why spend a life in anger, regret or mediocrity? What a waste when looking back. And since death renders everything meaningless, every man, woman and child was imbued with a single, simple thought. Why not live a life that matters?

✻   ✻   ✻   ✻   ✻

A figure lay on a tropical shoreline lapped by a warm sea. A tongue was licking his face, trying to summon him to consciousness. The waves rolled in to the deserted beach and the sun shone warmly overhead, infusing his limbs with its heat. It seemed as though he would not awake, but the tongue persisted with certain knowledge, and eventually its efforts were rewarded.

When the figure opened his salt-stung eyes, he saw a dog leaping, ecstatic at having woken his master. His mouth was parched and he ached all over. He could barely move for fatigue. He dragged himself up the shore, the dog pulling on the rags of his clothes to urge him on.

He must have fallen asleep. When he awoke the sun was lower in the sky, but the heat was still intense. The dog was barking, bounding about the beach. 'Easy boy,' he managed to croak, as the dog's excitement intensified. With a superhuman effort he forced himself to his knees. There was nothing to excite the dog's interest, just miles of steamy shoreline. He looked out across the ocean, raising his hand to his forehead against the sun. The dog couldn't control himself and started to run around in circles.

Tancredi had no idea where he was or what had happened. He felt sure his ragged condition meant he was alive. People didn't enter the after-life filthy, being licked by a dog. His last thought had been of Cocomo on the white swan. Then there was a flash and a falling through darkness. A dozen thoughts raced in his head, coalescing into the most fantastical. Perhaps there was something magical about the supernova and somehow he'd been saved.

He looked down the shoreline for Kasbek; he was leaping for joy beside
two little figures running in his direction. One was a boy with a galaxy
of freckles and glasses just like his, the other a girl in a yellow
and brown shuka. Beyond them, in the distance, his eye
was drawn to the silhouette of a woman against
the sunlight. She was walking down the
beach towards him, her black hair
billowing in the tropical
breeze.